Shelsley Beauchamp

Nelly Hamilton

Vol. 1

Anatiposi

Shelsley Beauchamp

Nelly Hamilton

Vol. 1

Reprint of the original, first published in 1875.

1st Edition 2024 | ISBN: 978-3-38282-857-8

Anatiposi Verlag is an imprint of Outlook Verlagsgesellschaft mbH.

Verlag (Publisher): Outlook Verlag GmbH, Zeilweg 44, 60439 Frankfurt, Deutschland
Vertretungsberechtigt (Authorized to represent): E. Roepke, Zeilweg 44, 60439 Frankfurt, Deutschland
Druck (Print): Books on Demand GmbH, In de Tarpen 42, 22848 Norderstedt, Deutschland

NELLY HAMILTON.

BY

SHELSLEY BEAUCHAMP,

AUTHOR OF

"GRANTLEY GRANGE."

"Trust not appearances.   Good often is
Where evil seems to be."

In Three Volumes

VOL. I.

London:

TINSLEY BROTHERS, 8, CATHERINE STREET, STRAND.

1875.

CONTENTS.

————◦◦◦————
·

CHAPTER I.

CHAPTER II.

CHAPTER III.

CHAPTER IV.

CHARLES DICKENS AND EVANS,
CRYSTAL PALACE PRESS.

CONTENTS.

—◦◦◦—
.

CHAPTER I.

CHAPTER II.

CHAPTER III.

CHAPTER IV.

CHAPTER V.

CHAPTER VI.

CHAPTER VII.

CHAPTER VIII.

CHAPTER IX.

CHAPTER X.

CHAPTER XI.

CHAPTER XII.

CHAPTER XIII.

NELLY HAMILTON.

CHAPTER I.

THE HAMILTONS OF EYMOR.

The Hamiltons of Eymor—a small hamlet on the borders of Herefordshire—were, by their position and property, the chief people of that district. They were six in family— father, mother, an elder brother and sister, and two younger children; and they lived at Eymor House, that was placed at the summit of a long green glade closed in by woods, and with high hills behind it.

Of larger dimensions than its name would indicate, it was a residence whose size and situation seldom failed to excite the attention of the passengers and the comments of the coachman, when the horses of the royal mail on the old coach-road below it were allowed breathing time up the steep bits by the dingles ; while the scarlet-coated guard awoke the echoes of the woods by the musical "Hey O chivey ! Hark forward, hark forward tantivey !" that he used to give on his horn, as a compliment to John Hamilton as they passed between his fox-covers.

Few indeed were they who drove along that road who did not take note of the house, and the beauty of its surroundings ; and even in later years, when the quick-stepping bays were seen no more, and the two old grey horses of the once-a-week carrier were the most important animals on the road—by virtue of the van they drew—it was still made a point of; for the driver, Noah Claypole, had always his little say ready, for the benefit of any stranger who might chance to be travelling with him.

"Jolly John's plaace, mum," he would remark, as he pointed with his whip towards it—"one o' the good oud sort; they be scaarce now. A be a rare un, he be. Ef yer goos to lor, an has him o' the Bench, youn ha justice done yer. Saame o' the Board. Ef he be theer youm roight, roighter nor youm be wi' the tother un, him as lives a thun Hawthorns theer, the miller's plaace— oud Jemmy Pinchem, mum, a hard-bitten un, as be no mon's friend, bad luck to him! Come up, hos. That be it, mum, yander, atwixt the loimestun quarry an the church, as yer sis the oud tower on it aboove the trees theer. Pop-pit! yer laazy brute, whoy dunna yer pull when a hits tha?

"Is, mum, a be a werry well-to-do sort

o' a mon, be Muster John. That be all his plaace up theer, an these 'oods, an them filds an hop-yards; an them two farms as well, as yer sis theer, up under the Ship Walk,—Eymor's Ind, an the Cherry Orchard; good-sorted uns them—as be theer, both on em, Muster Hemmin and Meyster John Gilbert. An that theer un as ye sis to the left on em, close under thun 'ood, the big fox-cover, that be another o' hisn—the Fox Farm— wheer Meyster Fred Freeman lives, as is a smart young blood, mum, as hunts a dale, an comes out in a red coat loike Meyster Frank an his feyther.

"An theer, yer can just catch the smoke on it a curlin up fro' the dingle under thun 'ood, a bit o' un orchardin plaace, that be hisn too, wheer oud Gaarge Lawson lives, mum, him as used to live in Upperton, but he wan burnt out. An that be oud Ood's mill, mum, yander, anant the bridge, as goos over

the Tame, as twisses aboot theer most on-
mercifully as it coomes down the walley.
An theer be the Lodge Farm as belangs to
the mill; we be jist in soight on it. Well,
Meyster Eddut lives theer, Eddut Warrilow,
as manes havin the darter, as thun oud mon
be heavy; uz saaved a dale. And theer's
the inn as we be a comin to, The Eymor
Arms, as has alleys a drap o' good, mum; as
a knows the brewer.

"An that theer's the Lodge wheer yer
sis the droive goo. An a werry pratty
droive it be too, mum; it twinies up
through thun 'ood to thun house, and be a
moighty saavin to the young Miss o' the
steep pitch theer, as be no joke for her pony
or the carridge, cos it be mostly laaid wi
stones, as a sorter drag for thun osses, as
they says be alleys that full o' oud banes—
they be done so well—as ood be ockard ef
they rund awaay, as they moight an offen,

an do some damage, as the turn at the bottom be stip; an Mrs. Tyler, mum, as lives at the Lodge, hur be that narvous, as hur haves hur family quick."

"Aye, theer be Miss Nelly thin—come hup Pop-pit, we mun git on a bit; how laazy yer be this marnin; yer lets Dobbin do all the work, yer do, darn yer body! come hup then, ool yer," said Noah, as he hit him over the back a good one,—"yander, mum, on the black pony, along o' Meyster Frank, an thun nipper. I alleys carries for they. Hur's got a parcel or a summut for ma a reckun. A don't nivir not loike to chaarge hur nothin, I don't, nohow, hur be sich a noice un; but hur oona ha' it though, hur oona, for hur'l shaake her pratty ed, an say, 'No, Meyster Noah, a shanna suffer it; yer han to git yer livin, and uz a dale o' trouble to yer.' Lord love her, mum, but it be a raal pleasure to waait on hur. Hur dunna kneow how glad I be to saarve her."

Thus would old Noah run on if he had any listener; aye, and by the hour together, never tired, as he jogged on at his usual pace of four miles an hour, of descanting on the Hamiltons; the name they had in the neighbourhood, and the many good qualities that were so generally ascribed to "dear Miss Nelly."

It was strange how this young girl—but twenty years of age—had won the hearts of all those simple people; strange, too, that her father, mother, and her brother Frank should each be spoken of as "poor folks' friends;" for, though wealth was theirs, they were no squanderers, nor bid for popularity with cash. Of that they spent they never made a talk: of that they did you never heard them speak; but that they lavished on all those deserving could not be hidden;

for, rough and rugged though a rustic be,
he is seldom proof against a constant kindness, words, ways, or acts; and thus it was,
through kind and friendly feelings, and homely
ways, that brought them close together; there
was not one in pretty Eymor village who
failed to speak well of the Hamiltons.

That "Nelly"— Ellen — Hamilton, who
was the eldest daughter, should be thus the
favourite she was with each person in the
place was not, however, to be wondered at,
when you came to know her, for her own
good qualities were apparent; and the more
so perhaps that she had not been gifted with
personal beauty; for though she was a well-
grown girl, with healthy colour and with rich
brown hair, handsome she certainly was not,
nor even pretty; yet her father's description
of her as "my good plain girl" was scarcely
justified, for there was mind in her counte-
nance, gentleness in her eyes, and such a

sweetness and tenderness in her very voice
that made her face worth a score of pretty
ones, for it was always attractive.

Joyous as a child, and just as innocent,
with a frank, sweet, happy look and soft
grey eyes, she long had been the loved one
of the village, for smiles accompanied her;
and her ready sympathy and kindness for her
poorer neighbours made her, with her sunny
manner, a welcome visitor at every cottage.

Genuine to a degree, and never so happy
herself as when she was contributing to the
happiness of others, she counted her friends
by the number of her acquaintances, for all
who knew her were fond of her, and they
liked her thoroughly. Too impulsive for shy-
ness, and too real for affectation, she was
sufficiently sensible to be free from primness
and prudery, and too lady-like to be fast or
forward.

Good - hearted and good - natured, always

cheerful and never idle, her household duties were a pleasure to her; for, lightened by the music of her voice, work was no work to her. A source of happiness in her own home, she was a treasure to her mother; and as she was the best of daughters, her father's praise of her was amply justified; but she had indeed the good word of all around her, for none could say ill of her.

Frank Hamilton—a fine good-looking fellow and three-and-twenty—was just such another, a worthy brother of such a sister, well-liked by all; for with plenty to see to, he was too much interested in the daily duties of the farm and the surroundings of his own home to think much of himself; and as his own personal identity therefore did not trouble him, it was never made prominent to others. With good general information, business aptitude, a knowledge of the world, and sound sense, he had sufficient self-reliance for decision of character. Orderly himself, open, straightforward, and independent, he heeded the carpings of the small minds as little as he did the praises of the feeble ones. Full of pluck and full of daring, with a straight look for his fellow men, and firm and resolute, he was yet as sensitive as a woman at distress, and as tender as a mother in relieving it.

The farmers spoke well of him, and the cottagers liked him, for, manly to all men, gentlemanly to all women, and child-like to children, he was kind to the poor, considerate to the work-people, and courteous to all : hence it was that Frank Hamilton was a general favourite.

John Hamilton, the father, whose cheerful looking face was a true index to his character, was a well-built man of fifty years of age, tall, stout, and muscular ; with curly hair that was still brown, and with a good thick beard that was just grey-sprinkled. The

prefix of "Jolly"—"Jolly John Hamilton"—
as given to him in the neighbourhood, was
an apt one; but it applied less to any special
jovial habits belonging to him than to the
habit he had of always looking "on the
bright side" of things; for no matter what
happened, or what trouble came upon him,
he had always a saving clause in its favour,
if no more than "it might have been worse."
To try to see things in their right light was
a rule with him; and if even there were no
bright side, visible to him at least, in any
new trial that came upon him, he acccpted
the position without a murmur, for he had
faith and trust; and a firm belief, therefore,
that whatever is sent us to bear is sent for
our own good. Hence it was that, happy
in his family, happy in his trust—his trust
in Him who ordereth—grumblings and com-
plainings were unknown to him; and his
cheerful manner communicated itself to his

workmen, who worked well and worked heartily, for the kindness and encouragement of good words they always had from him.

As one of the guardians of the parish the poor had much to thank him for ; and as a magistrate, when justice had to be done, mercy was not forgotten. A good man himself, and no man's enemy, an excellent father, a considerate master, and a kind landlord, "Jolly John" was a man well-respected and much looked up to ; and his name stood high in the county, for the name of Hamilton had never been sullied by him or his predecessors.

Of Ellen Hamilton, his wife, it may be sufficient to state that she was a good, motherly woman, of five-and-forty, fair-featured and comely; with whom the world went well so long as she obtained,—through Mary Moss, the keeper's daughter,—a brisk sale for her eggs, and a fair price for her butter, and there was a good demand at market for her ducks and her chickens. Industrious, good-tempered, and thoroughly domesticated, she was in all respects a worthy helpmate, who made home "home" for him who was her partner, and who, in her eyes, was such a husband as no other woman ever had, or could have.

Laura, "the pet," was a fair-haired girl of fourteen—"a love" as the old women said; and Robert, the youngest, was a lad of twelve. Three of their children were dead, a son and two daughters, John, Jane, and Marian, whose ages would have been at this date, twenty-five, seventeen, and fifteen respectively.

As her father had a very strong objection to public schools for girls, Nelly, until six months ago, had a governess at home—Miss Aymes—a clever woman, and one well versed in accomplishments, under whose able tuition she, Nelly, as she was quick and capable, made good progress; as did also Laura, who, bright and intelligent, was now taught by Nelly.

Robert, "Bob," "The Nipper," had been for a long time, however, past the management of Miss Aymes; her frequent efforts to instil into him good manners and good behaviour being altogether neutralised by his out-door propensities; which, coupled as they were with the constant companionship of the wagoner's lad, the mole-catcher, and the blacksmith, made him a perfect pickle, always in mischief, and up to tricks.

Unfortunately, he was in a measure encouraged in his naughty ways by his sister, as Nelly was very fond of him; and so she was always contriving excuses to get him out of scrapes. His father, too, added to the difficulty, by his admiration of the youngster's pluck, and his own intense belief in "muscle." Often and often did his mother urge that he should be sent to school, but it was in vain. "Get him hard first, mother," would his father say, "and then he will hold his own. If you force him too soon, he will be like a greenhouse-plant, a spurt and over. 'Healthy body, healthy brain,' remember that, mother. Wait till he is hard, and he will then make play, and learn more in one year than he would now learn in three." So, month after month would find Master Bob still at home, nominally taught by Miss Aymes; but really only learning that which would have to be driven out of him when the time came.

Bob's iniquities were, however, condoned by his father's theory, that made him, while frequently chiding the lad, for the look of the thing, to be inwardly rejoicing at the juvenile's precocity.

"What a young scamp it is, Frank," he

would say, delighted at some boyish prank he heard of; or, "what a plucky young beggar that lad is," when some unusually daring feat came to his knowledge. "We shall make a man of him, mother, depend upon it, he's hard," would be his comment, when Bob had been thrown by the pony an extra time or two, or had persisted in tackling the donkey till he could stick to her.

The falls that lad had in one way or other, and the number of times he came to decided grief were out of count; but short of broken bones nothing made a difference to him. In the birds'-nesting season he could tell you how many eggs were in each nest —he was never allowed to take them—all round the farm, and if the young rooks were getting forward for the rook-shooting, for he was as often to be seen at the top of the high elms as at the bottom of them.

And in all the other seasons, too, what there was to be told he could tell it; whether it related to the trout in the brook, the quice in the coppice, the hares or the rabbits, the young partridges or the pheasants; or even the number of cubs in each litter of young foxes; for Moss was keeper, and Bob was in his confidence.

At last, however, as even Nelly was obliged to admit that her young brother was getting " dreadfully vulgar," the time came when Mr. Hamilton had to yield; and for the past six months — since Miss Aymes left there—Bob had been to school in Worcester as weekly boarder, coming home each Saturday with one of their tenants, or with Frank in the dog-cart, and going back again on the Monday morning. The school was a good one, and as the head master was an old friend of the father, frequent communications passed between them; the general tenor of them being Bob's fighting propensities, and his dire hatred of books and school.

"Set him extra lessons if you like," would Mr. Hamilton reply, "but don't you stop him. The tasks will employ his brain, but he must not lose muscle. That is the one thing now-a-days to help a man through life, depend upon it. I believe in muscle, Charles. A quick, impulsive, and good-sorted lad like he is, if allowed to fight his way, will soon, by sheer pluck and manliness, make his way ; and he will in time get to take a lead in the school; for the stuff that is in him that now makes him hammer the lads, will, by-and-by, make you able to hammer into him what we want. Breed, condition, muscle, that's it, Charles. Let his pluck have vent, don't cow him, and he will then grow up manly and fit to face the world." So Charles Addison would smile, shake his head to himself as he read the letters, and murmuring "rod for his own back, depend upon it," let off Bob time after time with an extra lesson.

When, therefore, that young individual came home a week ago "for good," for the Christmas holidays, the improvement that was in him was far too slight to be visible; so Miss Nelly, as they were quite ashamed of him, was desired to take him in hand for the time being, as Laura's lessons had ceased for awhile, in consideration of the season and her brother's holidays; but when Nelly began "to preach," Bob walked off.

The only other occupants of Eymor House, besides the servants, were the two grooms, Charles Davis and old Joe Bennett; but William the wagoner and young Tom, the wagoner's lad—Timmis and Pritchett—slept there.

Amongst the live stock about the place were six horses and a black pony, White-face; so

named from the star on his forehead, the only
bit of white about him. He was Nelly's pet,
as she rode him constantly, and also drove
him in the pony-carriage. Her other pet was
Saucy Boy, a long low bay horse, that was
in the first loose-box; a good hack and a
clever hunter. In the boxes next to him were
her father's hunters—his brown horse Yeoman,
and his golden bay Gay Lad—and in the end
box was Firefly, that Frank rode, a jet black
horse, of great speed and a noted fencer. The
pony was in the hackney-stable with the
mare, Dapple Grey, that they used as farm-
hack and cover-hack, and drove in the dog-
cart. She too was good with hounds, and
clever; and the other occupant was Jack, the
brougham horse.

Out of the stable was the old saddle-room,
where Tom and old Joe blacked the boots;
and at the end of the stables, and opening
out of the last loose-box, by the cart-stables,

was the new saddle-room, where Charles, the smart young groom, learned songs by the stove, to sing to his lady love, Selina Morris, the flirty granddaughter of Hannah Pippit, to whom old Joe buckled-up on washing days, as she and Selina "washed" for the Hamiltons.

Besides the hackney-stable and the four loose-boxes, which had been built recently, there was a three-stall hunting stable, for the use of friends when they came there; and in addition to the sporting dogs and the greyhounds, there were also two terriers—Jip, the white fox terrier, and Dandie, the Dandie-Dinmont—who were quite as much pettied by Miss Nelly as were her doves and her love birds, and who always considered themselves slighted if she and the pony went off without them. Lion, the watch-dog, a fine fawn-coloured mastiff, he too expected from her his due share of notice, and as he was a noble faithful fellow, he always had it.

Gipsy, the donkey, a deep one, who would open all the gates to let the pony through, she too was another who looked for notice; and so was Peterkin, young Tom's magpie; though, as he did not deserve it, he was often slighted, for he was an artful bird and an improper bird, as he was not sufficiently particular in what he had to say, and there was too much emphasis in his language for polite society; shortcomings to be fairly attributed to his lack of moral teaching, through the misdirected tuition of Tom and the wagoner.

CHAPTER II.

NEW YEAR'S EVE.——NELLY AND THE RECTOR.

"THERE Master White-face!" said Nelly, as she jumped off her pony and patted him, "we are at home at last you see, and you have caried me famously; so I shall just munch you one bit, you dear old fellow, and then come and talk to you presently. Take him in, Joe," said she, when she had well cuddled him, "and I will bring him his crust when you've bedded him;" and as the old groom led him into the stable, she went on to the house with dog Jip; who, having been out with her and got dirty paws, declined to remain in the stall till his feet were dry.

"Oh won't you catch it, my lady!" cried Bob, who had come out on hearing the pony; "we hav'n't been waiting for you, have we?" "Punch his head, punch his head," said the magpie. "You rude boy," said Nelly, as she came through the wicket and stamped the snow off her boots, it is but just five o'clock, and you know it." "Hit him hard," said Peterkin. "Well, I just think, Miss Nell, you ought to have been back before this," was the reply; "I'm awful hungry, and I want my tea. Here, give us a kiss, I say, as you come under the misletoe; just one you know?" "I sha'n't," said Nell. "Shanna," cried the bird.

"Ah! I know," said Bob, as the door closed, and he stood with his back against the clock, while the girl helped her off with

her skirt and her jacket, "you want to keep
all the berries on it for cousin Fred to pick,
you do. He'll kiss you a good one, he will,
when he comes; you see if he don't now."
"I shall box your ears, sir, directly, you
young monkey." "Bob!" cried his mother,
"what are you about there? Come in, sir."
But Bob thought better of it, and went out
to old Joe and the pony; giving Peter a
swing as he went by him, and thus causing
the magpie to indulge in loose language; a
thing he was apt to do when provoked.

"I have not kept you waiting, mamma,
have I?" said Nelly, as Mrs. Hamilton came
into the kitchen. "No, dear," was the reply,
"there is no time over-past. There, change
your boots; I have got these warm and
ready for you. Jane, take Miss Ellen's skirt,
and see to it; and then bring in tea."
"Yes'm," said that domestic. "Well, Nelly,
so you have got back again, have you?

Why, you darling, how cold your hands are," said her father, as she came up to him, and raised his red face to her own. "There, sit you down, my girl, on my knee, and warm them." "Here, pet," said she, as she did so, "put my hat and gloves on the hall table, will you?" And Laura took them.

"Well, papa," said Nelly, smoothing her brown hair, and then warming her hands at the fire, "and what have you been doing with yourself all the evening?" "Out with Frank, dear, up the orchards, to knock a rabbit or two over. We killed but three though." "Then I dare say it was you I heard shoot as I came down the common."

"Very likely, my girl, for we are but just in. And how is little Bessie to-day?" "Better, thank you, papa. The doctor had just been there; but I fear, poor child, she will not last long—she is very thin. She

was so pleased with all I took her. I stayed
there some time, and read to her, or I should
have been back sooner. We put Master
White-face in the shed, and some bags on
him, so that he should not catch cold.
Little Johnny too, at the hill end, he is
better; and so is old Martha. I called on
her as I came back. She will send down
to-night for some milk and things." "All
right, Nell," said her father, "anything she
wants she can have; and so can all of them.
You know that, don't you?" "Yes, papa,"
said Nelly. "And what did the old women
say to your little presents?" asked Mr.
Hamilton. "Did they like them?"

"Oh yes," said Nelly, "so much. 'And
to think,' they said, 'of you making them,
Miss, your very own self, and for us old
women—cuffs and socks—and to be so good
as to buy us, too, a cross-over apiece! Why,
we shall each of us be warm night and day

now, that's certain.' Wasn't it fun, papa?
And then when I untied the other packet—
they carried capitally at the saddle-bow—
oh, they did exclaim! 'And tea, too,' they
said, 'for each of us, and sugar!' And
they looked so pleased, and they were all so
nice about it, that I was obliged to trot
away from one to the other as quickly as I
could, for I can't stand much of it, you
know, papa; my eyes get moist. But it is
nice to help them when one can, and especially at a time like this, is it not?" said
Nelly, looking up at him in her joyous way.
"It does make you feel so happy and so
cheerful, and—and so jolly; that's it, papa—
so jolly. Don't you think it does, now?"

"You would not be a Hamilton, Nell, if
it did not," said he. "And what about the
youngsters?" "Oh, they are all to have
theirs to-morrow. You must spare Tom,
please, papa, to come with me and the pony,

to carry them for me ; for what with the
donkeys' heads poking through in one place,
and the horses' legs in another, and the
shafts of the carts and the wagons making
a sticking out generally, I cannot wrap them
up anyhow. If you will, they can all go
then in one parcel—the Noah's arks, and the
soldiers, and the little farms, and all ; and
I can carry the picture-books.   There will·
be one or the other for each of them."
" That's right," said her father ; " you shall
have Tom when you want him."

" Now, Frank, tea, please," said Mrs.
Hamilton, calling up the staircase as she came
in from the kitchen.   " Coming, mother,"
said Frank ; and in a few minutes that good-
looking brother of hers pinched Nelly on the
cheek, and asked how her old women were,
and if the hop-drier was better and the
roadman's girl on the mend, and so many
other questions, that she was obliged to say,

"Now do let me have my tea first, Frank, and then I will tell you. Cut me off a crust, will you, for White-face?" "And one for me," said Bob, coming in and seating himself; "a good big piece, too, to start with, just while your hand's in. I don't like them thin pieces; they counts for nothin'." "Them counts for nothin', does 'em? Oh Bob!" said Nelly, "what a dreadful boy you are!" "Well, nothing, then; they counts for nothing." "They counts, eh? You horrid child!" "That's right, Nell; keep him up to it. You young nipper, you mend, don't you?" "Yes, pa," said Bob, promptly.

"I say, young gentleman," continued his father, "what was that I heard about you to-day—threatening to fight one of the lads in the rick-yard?" "It was that Austin's boy, pa, he sauced me; but if I do, I can lick him." "Bob!" cried Nelly, for she was

on to him in a minute, "if you don't leave
off that disgraceful word, I shall set you a
longer task than you fancy;" Nelly, as we
have said, being put in authority over Bob
during the holidays, to try to second the
schoolmaster. "You are a bad boy, Bob,"
said his father, trying to look serious, but
secretly rejoicing at the pluck of the
youngster; "don't let me hear again of such
goings on, or I shall have to whip you." So
Bob, "the nipper," munched up his crust in
a temper, and pushed over his plate for some
toast, getting a reproof from his mamma for
his most intemperate hurry.

As soon as tea was over, Nelly went to a
little store she had, and then, accompanied
by Dandie, proceeded to the stable, to see
after White-face, and to give him his crust,
and to mess with him, as old Joe, having
cleaned him thoroughly, had ceased to hiss
at him.

So the pony's ears were pulled, his soft flanks patted, his black nose rubbed, and he was cuddled all over; and then, after he had finished his crust, eating it out of her hand, and an apple that she gave him, she took a mane-comb from her pocket, and gave a final touch to the old man's handiwork. For be it known Miss Nelly had a mane-comb of her own, and she always carried it; for, as she said, "that dear old stupid pony will go poking about so at the banks for grass, that were it not for the comb I am sure when we are out he would not be presentable;" White-face having a longer mane than most ponies.

"Well, well! wait a bit; don't be so impatient," said Nelly, as the bay in the box kept neighing each time she spoke to the pony; "I shall not forget you, you beauty." Then, picking up the pony's legs, and being satisfied with their condition, she opened the door and went in. "Oh, that is very

naughty, Saucy Boy!" said she, as he put
down his ears, and playfully lifted a hind
leg. "I am sure you don't mean that now.
Come, turn over, sir! Oh, well, if you won't,"
said Nelly, "I must go round and creep
under you;" when having done so, and
emerged on the near side of him, she pushed
him to the other side of the stall, and began
to pet with him.

"Now, you naughty fellow, what do you
mean by your rude behaviour? Oh, I have
not got anything for you, I have given it
all to the pony. Well, now, what do you
think I have got there?" said she, as he
kept arching his neck and reaching after her
pocket, the light of the lantern catching on
him, and showing his bright bay coat to
advantage, as she turned back the clothing
to pass her hand over him, and to pat his
flank. "Well, then, will you carry me as
well the next time with hounds as you did

the last day, if I do find you something?
That was a day, that was, you know, for
each of us. Eh, will you?"

"Oh, you jolly pet," said Nelly, as he put
his head against her cheek, in reply to her,
and lovingly noddled his nose up and down;
"you make me love you. Then, I'll see.
Now, that is for dinner," said she, fishing
out a biscuit, "and this," as she gave him
some carrot, "is for dessert;" and Saucy
Boy crunched it up quickly, and put his
nose to her pocket for more. So the con-
tents of the pocket were emptied into the
manger, and a wisp of sweet hay pulled
from the rack for him; Nelly busying herself about him while he enjoyed it, and
making his mane and tail, that were loose
and glossy already, still more so, with the
mane-comb.

But while she was having a confidential
chat with him, preparatory to more loving,

and then a peep at the others, to see if they too were all right and comfortable—for her own satisfaction and her father's information—old Joe, who was busy with Tom in the saddle-room, opened the door, and said, "Theym a callin you, Miss. A thinks theer be company come." "Company?" said Nelly, "say I am coming then;" and taking leave of Saucy Boy, and giving a twist of the ear to Dapple Grey, a smack to White-face, and a pat and a pinch to Jack, as she came through the hackney-stable, she hurried to the house; Peter observing as she went by him, "Nelly, Maggit's a rogue," which was true.

"Where is my district visitor, my little Lady Bountiful?" said a cheery voice as she came in. "Oh, I am here, Mr. Arundell," said Nelly, answering for herself. "I have just been seeing to my pets, after a round in the parish. I hope you are quite well," said she, as she entered the room and shook hands with him. "And how are all at home?" said her mother. "You should have brought the ladies with you, Mr. Arundell." "Thank you, Mrs. Hamilton," said the rector, "my wife is much as usual, and she sent her good wishes to each of you. The girls, though, would have come with me, but they were afraid of the weather, for it looks like being a snowy night; and Clara has a cold, and Emma soon catches one." "Yes," said Frank, "I think there will be a downfall before the morning." "And how are you young people getting on?" said Mr. Arundell. "Oh, I'm getting on no end," said Bob, confidently, "at least —yes—that is, very well indeed, thank you," said he, correcting himself, as he saw his sister shake her head at him. "And I am too," said Laura, "ever so well; quite as well as Bob." "That's right, Pet, don't you

be outdone by Bob," said the parson. " I
don't mean to," said Laura.

So, settling down to Nelly, she and Mr.
Arundell had a long chat on parish matters
and the ailments of the invalids, to their
mutual satisfaction ; and then there was a
general talk on farm matters with the father
and Frank, and a gossip with the mother
about the poultry, and the pigeons, and the
dairy doings.

" Oh this is my chicken-tender and butter-
woman too," said Mrs. Hamilton, indicating
by her movement, Nelly, who was by her.
" And maid-of-all-work, I think, mother,"
said her father, " for there is not much that
she does not do." " But I like to be busy,"
said Nelly. "And like to do good," said
the parson. " I hope so," said she.

"But you surely will stay and have a bit
of supper with us, New Year's Eve and all,"
said Mr. Hamilton, as the rector got up to

go, after a long talk with Frank, who was his churchwarden, and a gossip with them all. "Not to-night, Hamilton, thank you," was his reply, "for we are expecting my lad Will by-and-by. Walton is gone in with the dog-cart; he said he would get away from town by the two-fifteen that reaches Worcester at six, so as to be with us to supper; he hopes to spend a week with us, and it is just chance work if he does not pick up nephew Harry at Oxford, and bring him with him, if they will let him off for that long. He is staying with some friends there—the Camerons—who own the new house he has taken near Holland Park; his studio, though, is in North Audley Street.

"That lad will do something to be talked of, one of these days, Hamilton. He had two pictures at the Academy this time, his first year there, and sold them both; and he tells me his pictures now are seldom long on hand." " Yes, I think he will," was the reply. " I saw his name mentioned in the papers, as that of a rising artist; and his pictures have been praised in the ' Art Journal ' and the ' Athenæum,' and also in the ' Guardian.' You ought to be proud of him," said Mr. Hamilton. " We are proud of him, for he is as good as he is clever; a very worthy young fellow, indeed," said his uncle, " though I say it. And how are you getting on with the painting, Miss Nelly ? "

But Nelly, from some cause or other, was blushing so deeply, that had not her handkerchief been let fall accidentally under the table, obliging her to stoop for it, Mr. Arundell must have noticed it. " Ah !" said he, in reply to her, when she came to the surface, " we shall have him with us, I hope, in April, after he has sent in his pictures;

and then you must again get some sketching together. I think he means to paint that old wainhouse of yours at the back. You must work with him, Miss Nelly, and watch him; it will improve you. He said, when he was last here—in October—that there was good work in your pictures, as you may know by their selling, and that all you needed was a little instruction now and then; and that I am sure he will be glad to give you, for I know you are a favourite." So Nelly blushed again, and changed the conversation.

" Come, Mr. Arundell," said her father, " sit you down a bit then, if you won't stay supper, and have one glass before you go, to keep the cold out, and drink to ' absent friends.' Touch the bell, mother, for some hot water." " Then one glass, Hamilton, for New Year's Eve."

"By Jove ! what a night it is ! here's

snow! Turn your collar up, parson," said Mr. Hamilton, as they came out on the lawn together; "it will be a regular blinder by the look of it." "Yes," said the rector, "and God help all poor wretches who have no roof over them." "God help them," said Hamilton, as they shook hands heartily and parted.

"Please 'm, I think the carol-singers are coming. I heard the gate go, now just," said the girl, as she brought in glasses after supper, for good healths all round and a good New Year.

> "When shep-herds watched theer flocks boy noight,
> Aa-all saated on the groun."

"Aye, there they are," said Mrs. Hamilton; "put the kitchen door open, Jane, and tell them to come in under the pent-house. We shall hear them better there, and they will be out of the wind." "They are Gould's three youngsters, I think," said Frank, "by

the sound of them; and that young Jack
Smith and Dick Whittaker, and the two
Butler lads." "Now, Bob," said Nelly, "if
you are going out, just you put your cap
on, sir, and don't you baffle them. They
will do it very well if you will let them
alone." But in a minute or two an extra
voice was added to the others, and that so
noisily that Bob was had in immediately.
"They don't do it amiss, do they, papa?"
said Laura, who was sitting up late for that
night only. "No, my pet, I think they
sing it very fairly. Ah! that is another old
one," said he, as they shouted,

> " God bless the meyster of this house,
> Like-wise the mis-tress too."

"How many of them are there, Frank," said
his father. "I'll see," said he. "Seven, and
it's snowing," was the report, "and cold
enough to pinch your nose off." "Then call
them in," said Hamilton, "and what we have

for them, they shall have by the fire. Tell them to sit down on the settle, and to pipe up."

So the youngsters were had into the kitchen; which was as well, for Peterkin, who was in his warm corner over the furnace at the end of the pent-house, where he was nightly placed, had been woke up suddenly by the noise, and was then making use of very bad language; and the blending of sacred and profane in that manner was not particularly edifying. Then when their stock of songs was sung, a new shilling each was given to them, and after they had all had some plum-cake and a drop of hot elder wine, they went on down the hill to the rector's.

"Ten minutes to twelve, Nelly," said her father, as he looked at his watch, some time after Bob and Laura had dropped asleep; so put the wrappings on, girl, and you, mother, and rouse these youngsters, will you, and wrap them up. Now, you women," said he to the servants in the kitchen, "Where are the men?" "Young Tom is at the front, sir, with William," said the cook. "And old Joe," said Jane, "is out, sir, by the kid-pile." "And Charles is with him sir," said Emma. "Theym a arknin to the bells, mum," said Betsy, the scullery-girl, who wished to add her testimony to that of the housemaid's. "Oh, well, come along then," said Mr. Hamilton; and the front door was unfastened and thrown wide open, Frank calling to the men.

And while they all stood there on the steps, listening to the bells, as the sound of them, slowly tolling, came up to them from the valley—tolling for the old year that was ending — the clock struck twelve, and the bells clanged out, joyously, merrily, quickly, and lustily; and master and servants, mistress and children, wished each other heartily, "health and all happiness," for the year that was in.

"Lawsons, I see, are just off," said Mr. Hamilton, after they had stood there some time, and he looked down on Landimoor, in the woods below him, as a light showed there in the upper window. "It is to be hoped old George is in," said Frank; "Charles says he was at the cider-shop when he came by, and he thought he was getting on a bit." "Ah! I am afraid," said his father, "George is going the wrong way. Was young George with him?" "I should say not," said Frank, "as he told me this morning, when I was down at their place, that he was going over the hill to Upperton, to a dance there; so he would not be likely I fancy to be home till morning." "I suppose they have never had any tidings of Jessie?" "Never," said Frank. "Poor girl!" said Hamilton.

And as the last bank of grey clouds scattered, and the moon, now almost at the full, shone out above the woods, the bells chimed sweetly, and the stars came out, first here and there, then clustered, keen and glittering; for the night was clear and the snow had ceased, and all the sky was one cold sweep of blue.

" Well," said jolly John Hamilton, as they took a last look at the lights in the village and the white world that was below them, " we must turn in now, mother; so may the Lord send us a lucky year, and God bless everybody."

Yes, God bless everybody, John Hamilton; and that poor girl who lies there in the snow, with her white face turned to heaven !

CHAPTER III.

EYMOR VILLAGE, AND THOSE WHO LIVED THERE.

THE next morning ushered in the new year winterly, for snow was everywhere; and as Nelly drew back the curtains as she was dressing, and looked out upon the woods, the long green glade was white as any sheet, and on the snow-topped trees the rooks were silent, dropped over there from their own rookery. A hare was squatted, too, within the garden, and rabbits that were scampering on the lawn, scattered the snow, like white dust, in the laurels, which bent beneath the weight the night had brought; and robins on the walks were waiting crumbs. All round was shining snow, pure white, and crispy; above it, blue, and in the distance, grey—a slatey-grey, and marked about with orange, just where the round red sun was slowly rising through the dull haze that hid the distant hills.

And when Nelly, who was always up before her mother, had come down-stairs and busied herself about the house, she put on her hat and went out to the stables. "Marnin, Miss," said the magpie. "Good morning to you, Peter; and the same to you, Joe, and many happy years," said Nelly, as the old man came out of the saddle-room. "You must take the pony to the shop, please, to have him turned-up a bit, for this weather looks like lasting; and about these banks, frost nails are of no use, none whatever. Oh, very well," said she, as the bay and the pony both neighed as they heard her, "I will just come to say how-d'ye-do, but I cannot stay now, you know; I am busy." So she went in, smacked White-face and patted Saucy Boy, and put her cheek to each of them, just to satisfy them, and then flitted back again to see to breakfast.

"Nell," said Bob, who was in the kitchen, looking up at the mistletoe, "I'm a-countin' the berries at the bottom of the bush; and I shall count 'em again when old Fred's been. Ten from fifty, and forty's left; that'll be about the lot of it this time to-night, I know. He's safe to have ten at least—a berry a kiss: he's a brick for kissin', he is," said Bob, knowingly. "Bob," said Nelly, "mind I don't set you a lesson, sir, you slangy boy." "Well, isn't he now? And I know somebody else who likes it too. Ah!" said he, "I saw you, Miss, both of you, on Christmas-day. Wer'n't the berries a-goin'

it ! "   " You wicked boy," said his sister,
"how can you say so ?   I cannot understand
how you can even think of such a thing,
such a dreadful thing."   " Well," pursued
Bob, " I know this, Nell : I've kissed young
Polly, and she's kissed me, oh ever so often,
and we haven't found it 'dreadful.' "

"And who, in the name of all that's
horrible, is Polly?" enquired Nelly, who was
aghast at such revelations.   " Why, Polly
Everill, on the common, to be sure," said
Bob.   " You little monster ! " said Nelly.
"To think of such goings on.   Oh you
dreadful boy ! And what do you suppose is
to become of you as you grow up?"   "Oh, I
know," said Bob, jerking his head knowingly.
"I shall go a-huntin', like pa, and jump the
hedges, and be a farmer."   " There ! you go
off this instant, sir," said Nelly, seeing that
talking to him was useless, " or I will set
you a lesson, you little manikin ; you are

even worse than I thought you were." So, as the cook just then came into the kitchen, Bob walked off, leaving Nelly busy with the bacon.

"Nell," said he, as she came into the breakfast-room, "I shan't do a lesson if you set it me. I'm a-goin' a-rabbitin'." "You will." "I oona." "You 'oona,' you little precocity?" "Well, I won't, then." "Hillo, Bob, what is that you won't do?" said his father, as he came in with Laura. "Oh, nothing," said Nelly; "he is only on with his nonsense, papa." So Bob again escaped, and chuckled accordingly, and kicked Nell afterwards under the table, as much as to say, "That's one to me, Miss."

As soon as breakfast was over, Tom was ordered to tidy himself, and to be in readiness to go with Miss Ellen; and Nelly sending Laura for "the things," commenced to sort them out and to wrap them up. But while

she is thus engaged, and old Joe is getting
the pony ready to carry her and her presents
to their destination, we will just glance at the
surroundings of her own home, and then have
a look round at the common and the village,
to see some of the places where she is about
to go to; the homes of the cottagers and the
work-people.

Eymor House, as we have mentioned, was
situated on high ground, above some woods,
and under long green hills. It was a red
brick house, with white stone dressings, and
lengthy, large, and roomy ; the only old bits
about it being at the back of it, where they
were incorporated with the modern structure.
The greater part of the moat, one long length
of it, was however still there, as a provision
in case of fire, and for the benefit of the ducks
and the moor hens; but just in the front it
had been filled up, when the terrace garden
was formed, that was below the lawn and

above the long green glade; from which it
was separated by a deep sunk fence.

This glade, "the green valley" as it was
called, was a hollowed sweep of turf, that on
either side sloped downwards from the woods,
and was closed in at the bottom by the
dingles. These woods, which were half a mile
or more in length, and joined up to the
gardens by the house, gates opening from them
to the shrubberies, lay upon two high ridges
that shelved down to the valley near the road;
and they sloped over them on the outer side,
to slanting pasture land, and corn and barley.
And where they met the dingles, hop-yards
lay, and long green meadows, that ran up to
the bridge that crossed the brook, near to the
turnpike, where the main road turned down-
hill to the village; a little hamlet lying in a
hollow below the avenue from Eymor House.

A team road from the village through the
fields, led to a farm, hemmed in by orchards,

deep down in the dingles, with a foot-road from the bridge through hop-yards to it, and a bridle-road above it through the wood. The farm was Landimoor, and Lawson lived there, a place of Hamilton's.

And on the other side, the left-hand side as you looked from the house, another road, lined like its fellow with some old elm trees, sloped steeply to the coach road in the valley. From this steep road "the drive" turned at the lodge, and wound up through the wood to Eymor House. Near to the lodge lived Peter Bell, the roadman, whose only child, a tiny pale-faced mite, was under Nelly's care, and very ill. Beyond it was the lodge farm by the brook, near to "The Eymor Arms" that faced the road; and by the road between there and the village were Purdey's shop, and several scattered cottages, where people lived who worked upon the farms.

At the back of Eymor House, behind the

buildings, was a walled-in garden and a rookery—the thickened centre of the avenue, where both roads met. Two lanes went from there, a right-hand one, that wound between the ash-beds to the common, and one upon the left, that led to the Cherry Orchard, and Eymor's End, and went on to the Fox Farm by the cover—three farms of Hamilton's— and branched off to the Home Wood, near the house. Deep in this wood lived Thomas Moss, the keeper, and under it the mole-man, Aaron Woodruff, who acted as earth-stopper in the season; the wood end, that was nearest to the common, making a crescent sweep, that screened the house, and sheltered sundry orchards, and the paddocks.

The common, lying on the hill-side slope, was high above the dingles and the brook, and threaded by footpaths, and in dips and hillocks; one mass of ferns, and hawthorn trees, and gorse. The top, and just one side, was cleared for cottages, and thick turf grew there, as also at the bottom, by the brook.

In the upper row, a cluster of six cottages, lived Smith, Gould, Davis, Pritchett, Jones, and Austin, who all worked on the farm; as also did their wives, when they were wanted; Mrs. Pritchett being young Tom's mother, and Mrs. Davis, Charles's; and it was little Johnny Austin, in the last of these cottages at the hill end, that Nelly spoke of the night before; and his brother, "young Nat," was the lad Master Bob wanted to fight in the rick-yard; and the hop-drier, old Jones, whom she also named, and whose sons worked at Eymor, he lived next door to him. Gould's lads and Smith's lads were amongst the carol singers, with young Dick Whittaker, and the Butlers, whose people lived on the slope of the common, by Badsey and Lewis, in four thatched cottages; and Hill, and Price, and Raybould, occupied the

three other houses that were near the
brook, and just beyond the little bridge that
crossed it.

On the bank, to the right of the bridge,
and beyond the end of the common, where
the brook entered the dingles, were three
more cottages, of stone, and brick, and thatch,
like the rest of them. These were tenanted
by Mrs. Everill, whose rosy daughter was
the " Polly" with whom Master Bob had
been flirting—old William and Mary Morton,
and their granddaughter, Priscilla—" Prissie"
—a buxom damsel of two-and-twenty, and
betrothed to William, the wagoner; and the
widow Benbow, whose child, a consumptive
girl of twelve, was the " Bessie" named by
Nelly; and young Tim—Timothy—was her
little brother.

Most of these people—the men-kind at
least, and several of the women, as also
some in the village—worked for Mr. Hamil-

ton, on the farm he occupied, or on those held by his tenants; and it is because we shall be meeting with many of them in the course of our narrative, that we here allude to them.

At the bottom of the bank below the avenue, where the road went through the village, there was a side-road which branched off to the right past the rectory, and went on by the Hawthorns,—where Minchem lived that old Noah talked about, — the Bank Farm, where Corbett lived, and by Papworth's, at the Poplars, to the quarry, and thence to the main road.

At the corner of this side-road, and near the rectory, was the church, the school-house and the school; and the Church Farm, where Tom Burgess, Frank Hamilton's friend, lived. Beyond it, going on into the village, was "the shop." Mr. and Mrs. Wallace lived at the school-house, and Mrs. Martha

Haden and her daughter Patty kept the shop, which was also the post office, and the general gossiping-place for the whole village. Opposite the shop, two bridle-roads turned—the one through the gorse at the back of the Bank Farm, to join the lane between Eymor's End and the Fox Farm, and the other through the fields to the hills. By this road, and above the quarry, were three stone cottages, where Shepherd the hedger, Wainwright the thatcher, and old Jem Webb the fisherman, lived.

Next to the shop lived Isaac Walker, the clerk and gardener; and by him, Old Tom Norton the cow-leech; a very useful man in the place, as he was also well up in horses and their ailments — a little rosy-faced, white-haired, thick-set man, who sang a good song and was capital company; and who was therefore in great requisition at all feasts and festivals. He was a widower, though, according to his own account, he had hard work to remain so, "for half the women, and most o' the young chits on that side the country, were dying for him!"

On the other side the way, close to the by-lane that came down from the Hawthorns, was Byfield's place, the pig-killer; and beyond it Burton's, the blacksmith, whose shop adjoined his house. At the back of Burton's, where a little trig went across the fields, were several cottages—a row of five, then two single ones, and past the stile two more. Hannah Pippit and her granddaughter lived in one of these, and old Peplow, the head ringer, in the other —much to Charles, the groom's, annoyance, as whenever he was taking a fond fare-well of Selina, after seeing her safe home on washing days, or meeting her there whenever he had the chance of it, old

Abraham—who always seemed to them to be coming home or going out that way—would be sure to be wanting to get over the stile, and so disturb the pair of them; but as the path ended at his own garden there was no help for it.

On the high ground above these cottages was The Poplars, with a rough road to it from the long church lane. Papworth lived there, who had the ox team; and to the right of it, but at a lower level, was Danks's farm, Dingle Wood, a very fruity place, and cheap at the money. Down the road, near the entrance to the village, was the cider-shop—Amphlett's; and on either side the road, between there and the turnpike—that William Ford kept—were some more cottages; as also some straggling ones in the fields adjoining; the only ones, however, that it is necessary to specify being those by the hop-yard, where Roberts, Potts, and Turner lived, three of the

ringers, the best fellows to work that Mr.
Hamilton had, and famous mowers.

The mill, from which the people about
there had their flour, was, as old Noah pointed
out, near to the bridge that crossed the river;
and as the river ran obliquely there for some
distance, and the mill was but a little way
down the bridge lane, it formed, with its
foaming weir adjoining it, a picturesque object,
as the house by the mill was covered with
ivy, and some fine old elms were at the back
of it; and Jabez Wood, the miller, who lived
there, was fond of flowers, so there was always
bright colour about it while flowers lasted.

It was to his good-looking daughter, " little
Jenny," that Edward Warrilow was engaged;
and people did say that as he and Jenny
were always courting up the meadows in the
twilight, or hanging about the bridge in the
moonbeams, before very long Abraham Peplow would have the order for " a peal." So

the Eymor Arms' folks—Mr. and Mrs. Dun-
niman—kept an eye to the good condition
of their October brewings. "Master Frank"—
Frank Hamilton—was always "on with him"
about it; but as Warrilow was a very good
fellow, he took it all in good part, which was
the best way, for the people of the village
were constantly meeting with him and Miss
Jenny in the fields, and the woods, and the
hop-yards; and as they naturally said, "Moind
now ef so be as theer baynt a weddin' agate;
fur a oodna hang to her loike that theer ef a
didna mane summut;" adding, as their testimony to his character, "fur it be uproight
and down straaight as be Meyster Eddutt."

Having now mentioned the chief people in
Eymor village with whom we shall have to
deal, we will just glance at the surroundings,
and quit the subject.

As seen from the old coach-road, Eymor
House was the chief feature, for the village

was hidden; and it was only as you ascended the long steep hill that led to the breezy downs above it that even the church was visible. That, like most of the village churches in that district, was an old one, with a short thick tower, yews, ivy, and lich-gate; and also, as a matter of course, the ever-present mounting-block, which is so significant of days gone by, when the state of the roads obliged all the outliers to ride to church, if indeed they wished to arrive there decently.

Of the farms that were scattered about there, four belonged to the lord of the manor, four to Mr. Hamilton, and three—the Mill Farm, the Lodge Farm, and The Hawthorns— to old Jabez Wood, the miller. The cottages on the common too were Hamilton's, and also the one—the old roadman's—that was by the lodge.

Eymor, with its tinkling brooks, and its

wealth of foliage, in dingle, wood, and copse, was a pretty place enough at any time; but in the autumn, when its russet tints got such a good backing of purple, and green, and grey, from the long high hills at the back of it, it certainly was a very pretty place; especially when you looked at it from the high ground, so as to take in the village, and the church and the rectory, for all the ground about there was undulating; and the farms were so clumped, and the long green hills so high, with the gorsy common, and its cottages, and the Home Wood, and the fox-cover creeping up the slope of them, that none but those who saw it daily could fail to be pleased with it.

The summer, however, was the time when it attracted most notice, for then the people came out of the hot and dusty towns, to go upon its breezy hills to get fresh air, and see the country round: for the beauty of the views from "Eymor Sheep-walk" was too well known to be passed over; and so the gipsy-parties that came there, season after season, were a source of considerable revenue to the Eymor Arms people, and also of un-limited sixpences to Aaron the mole-man; at whose cottage, under the wood, the kettles were boiled, and his own services accepted as guide and panorama-man, for he could give you chapter and verse for all that was to be seen there.

"The power o' hills, the Tame walley, an the Welsh mountings, an all the plaaces i' thun 'oods as be good for flowers, Miss; loikewoise the twiney paths as be tangled hup loike, as yer may be plased to know on, in case yer young mon may be ooth yer; when in coorse, Miss, lookers-on bayn't waanted, as two be coompany an three be none, when courtin's agate, as be nat'ral."

At the back of Aaron's house, too, was a
grass-plat—"a lorn," he called it—which, as
he always informed the ladies, he "batted
down wi' his own blessed 'ands o' puppose;"
so that they should have a dance if they
wished it, as he liked the ladies; "an a
bower convaniant for 'em to rest theerselves
in, an wheer they could be talked to comfortable loike by the young gen'lemen, as
'ood be agrayable to theer feelings, no doubt,
an a makin' o' things pleasant all round."
So that what with Aaron's cottage, the civility
of his wife, Rebecca, and the little attentions
of pretty Mary Moss—Mrs. Hamilton's mar-
ket-girl—who would come down to help her,
the ladies of the party always fared well
there; and if the gentlemen wanted some
fossils from the quarry, or plants from the
woods, or fancied an hour or two at the
brook or the river, before returning home,
Jem the fisherman was at hand, and ready

—Jem and Aaron being cronies, who worked into each other's hands, and shared the spoil.

CHAPTER IV.

YOUNG BOB, AND BURT THE DOCTOR.

"Now Nelly," said her father, as old Joe brought White-face to the door, "the pony is ready, so if you have got the things together you had better be off, while it is fine, for I think we shall not be long before we have more snow. Take care how you go, Tom, and open the gates for Miss Ellen. Here, sling this round your shoulders, and never mind the magpie; he is saucy enough already, so don't make him worse." "Is, meyster," said Tom, as he put the leather round his neck, and pushed the packages,

that were fastened at either end of it, back
under his armpits, so as to have his hands
free; "uz see to 'em." "Were those right,
Nell, did you count them?" said Mr. Hamilton,
alluding to sundry new shillings that he
had given her for the youngsters. "Yes,
thank you, quite right, papa; twenty-two,
just one a-piece," said Nelly. "Then be off
with you, and get back soon, and tell them
to be good children," said he, as he kissed
her. So Nelly started for her New Year's
Day distribution to the children of the cottagers; the old people, as we have stated,
having had their usual gifts on the previous
evening.

"Frank, shall you be Eymor's End way
this morning?" said Mr. Hamilton, as he
returned to the house, after watching Nelly
down the bank, and till she had turned on
to the common. "No, but I can go, father,"
was his reply, "if you want anything."

"Well, don't go on purpose, my lad, but if you are by there just look in the kiln, will you, and put the tools out. They are under the stairs there; we shall want them soon." Gilbert did not grow hops, as his was a dairy farm, but the hop kilns were there, as being handier in the picking for the land-lord, and less of a drag for his horses. "And if you see John, tell him when he has nothing better to do, to come up and have a rubber with us; he and Freeman, too, if you meet with him. He and Master Gilbert are getting quite stay-at-homes." "I think so, too," said Frank.

"Where's that lad Bob gone to?" "Up to the keeper's, I fancy, for he went under the rookery just now," said Frank, "and I heard the wood gate slap. I dare say he is there, or at Aaron's." "Confound the lad, he is always off with the mole-man or the keeper. What a pickle it is!" "I will look

in at the cottage, father, as I pass, and get
him come with me if I find him. I did say
something to him about rabbiting, but if I
drop on him, we can have a turn with
Gilbert at his place; if he is in, at least."
"Do," said his father. "What are the men
at, Frank?" "William and Benbow are up
the road, carting; I thought they had better
shift those road scrapings. And I put Wainwright on at that rick, where the thatch was
faulty. Shepherd I started with some trous
and hetherings, to make those places square
that the hounds knocked over; and Gould
is thrashing. The women are turnip-cutting;
and Price and Raybould," said Frank, "are
loading in the fold-yard. The others you
know about." "Yes; all right," said
Hamilton. "Then you are just off, are
you?" "As soon as I have been to the
stables. I thought, as Charles can manage
the horses, Joe might as well cut chaff till

Nell comes back; and then he and Tom can have a turn at our tops, in case they are wanted." "Not much chance, lad, of that just yet; for Apley Wood and Cobbler's Coppice, too, will have to slide, unless a thaw comes. If we can air our pinks at Hurtley Gate, on this day week, we shall be lucky. This snow looks lasting." "Well, don't wait for us, father, if we are not home to dinner; for if we should have a turn with the dogs at John's, we might stay there, and so bring him back with us." "Very well; but pick that lad up if you can," said Hamilton. "I will," said Frank.

Then, after seeing to the stables, he went on up through the orchards and the paddocks, to the Home Wood at the back, as he wanted to see Moss the keeper. Moss was out, however, but as Mary said she thought he was only gone to Woodruff's, Frank went there, and found him along with Aaron; and

Master Bob, too, who was in the cottage, handling the mole-traps, and talking to the wife, Rebecca. So, after a chat with them, Frank walked off Bob, and they went down the fields together to Eymor's End.

"Where's the master, Jack?" said Frank, as he met the wagoner's lad. "Well, sur, a wan i' the cowhus the last toime a sid 'm, a dressin' Daaisy, as Fillpaail goored this marnin'. Hur got i' her plaaice i' the boosey, sur, so Fill foighted hur, an gin˙ hur one; as hur be the master-cow, sur, an has the top stall. But mebbe, an perhaps, a be hup the grouns now, sur, somewheer a reckun; onles a be drapt in at oud Tummus Norton's aboat Dia-munt, as be had, sur; but the missis be in, hur's i' the fowl-hus, or the darree." "Well, Mrs. Wormington," said Frank, when he found her, "as usual, busy amongst the chickens. What a capital poultry-woman you are! Where's Gilbert?" "Jane!

which way did the master go just now?"
"Off to the gorse, mum; but the pig-killer,
Byfield, mum, as be just gone, he said as
he met him anant the Fox Farm." "Ah! I
daresay," said her mistress. "He said he
thought he should go sometime to-day, and
give Mr. Fred a look in. If you will come
in and have something, Mr. Frank, and you
Master Robert, I will send Jack for him."
"No, don't trouble, thank you; I want to
go into the kiln to put some tools out, and
then if he has not come back when I have
looked round the stock, we will go on up
the lane and meet him."

And they did so, as Bob was getting
dreadfully weary at nothing offering that
enabled him to be in mischief. Before they
reached the farm, however, they met them—
Freeman and Gilbert—so they turned back
with them. "Fred and I," said Gilbert,
"were just going to have a turn round the

hedgerows after those beggaring rabbits ; so you are just in time." "Very well," said Frank ; "it is an idle day with me, and it will suit this youth too ; in fact, we were going rabbiting together, but the governor wanted me to look in the kiln here for some tools. When are you fellows coming to have a rubber with us ?" "Oh, one of these nights," said Gilbert. "We'll look you up," said Freeman ; "never fear." "Well, do, and soon."

"Now, Mrs. Wormington, can you start us a bit of something for lunch ? What is there ?" "Well, pretty well for choice, Mr. John ; there's a lot in the larder. Shall I put the roast beef on, and the large pork pie ?" "Yes, do," said Gilbert, "or we shall never get through.it. You fellows can do pork pie, I think, can't you ? And some ale, Mrs. Wormington, too, please. What is this young shaver to have, Frank ? Our

ale is strong, and so is the perry." "Then
give him some cider." "I can drink ale,"
said Bob. "Not this ale, Bob; it will get
into your sconce, you young nipper, and
make you coxy. Be content," said Frank.
So the pork pie and the rest of the good
things there were done justice to; and then,
whistling for the dogs and telling Jack to
bring the ferrets, they started, with a good
stick each, thinking, as "the youngster" was
with them, they would let the guns alone,
for fear of accidents, Bob being an impetuous
youth, and apt to get where he was not
wanted.

"Where do we go to first, John?" said
Frank. "Into the paddock; there's a sprout
there," said· Gilbert, as he lit his pipe and
gave Frank a light. But there were no
rabbits at home there, for Brindle, after
listening with paw up, left Tartar to himself, to scratch and snuff if he had doubts

about it. The first place they tried in the Rough orchard was right, however, and old Brindle's tail was soon all that was to be seen of him; when Bob, who saw a chance to be doing something, went to him, and catching hold of it, lugged him out by it. Then letting Tartar in, he made Brin wait; but, rubbing his redded nose, Brin pottered off to what was, as he thought, the other outlet, where he put on his most deliberate look and waited patiently close by the side till called by Bob to have another innings and be dragged back again in the self-same way. "What the deuce are you at there, you young varmint?" said Frank. "Let the dogs alone, will you; they'll have you by the leg else, and serve you right, if you don't mind what you're up to." "But it isn't fair for one to have all the scratching," said Bob; "they ought to share alike." "Cut away this minute, you young monkey, and

come behind here. Do you think a rabbit
would bolt with you stuck there? "Yes,"
said Bob, " and then I should catch him."

" Jack," said Gilbert, " keep that dog
back. Quiet, Bob. Look out! he's close at
here. Loo, loo, a scut!" Then out and
off with springy jump goes Tartar, meets
Brindle turning, cannons, and both fall,
down to the bottom of the bank, through
brambles : the rabbit safe through the thorny
hedgerow, and away. "Confound you dogs!"
said Gilbert. " Here, Tartar! Brindle! Jack,
put a ferret in; we'll have fair play.
Another's here, just under where I am.
Keep these dogs back, Frank. Now then,
Fred, look out. Quick! here he comes.
Loo, loo, loo, Tartar! hi! Brindle." The
pace too quick for distance; Brindle snaps
him.

They tried the next place, both dogs
walked away; then hunted up the hedge-

row to the top, where Tartar was soon earthed, and Brindle on his side, hard on at roots, half smothered by the dirt that Tartar flung out. A speedy bolt, and both dogs through the hedge; Jack there, to turn — killed in the open. The grip to Brindle, but the kill to Tartar, so one and one. Then they went on into Cowcroft orchard, when out of the feg and stuff at the top of it they moved a hare, but stopped the dogs and put them through the rough grass in the centre, but did not find; nor did they further on, for the sprouts they tapped had not a rabbit in them. They put a jack-snipe up though in the rushes, as they went on by the pool side beyond there; and in the Hollow orchard they again found the rabbits at home, and got three—two with the ferrets, and the third a bolt; one each the dogs, the other was a tie, they fastening on the instant both together. Then Rye-grass orchard next; there they did well, but lost a couple through a quickset hedge; the rabbits did it, but the dogs hung in, so that made up to then just one to Tartar.

As they moved for the ash-bed, Sam came up—the rectory lad—with a message from the rector, to ask them down there for the afternoon, to have some skating and an evening after. He said he had been up to Mr. Frank's and to the Fox Farm, and the master told him to say they had ridged the croquet-ground and made a rink, and also swept the pool there in the meadow, and he and Master William hoped they'd come. So they sent word they would do so.

"Now then, Jack," said Mr. Gilbert, after they had tried another place or two, "festoon the rabbits, and then bring them on." "Festoon 'em, sir?" "Yes; slit through the thigh, between the sinews there; yes that, the right leg. That's it. Now push the left leg through it; there you are. Now put him on your stick and sling the others, the same as that one, and then follow us." Then shutting up the rabbiting, they got back home and spruced, had dinner, and went down; Nelly, who was a good skater, and who had also been invited, going there with Frank, as Fred, her cousin, had not arrived.

But though she was in the highest spirits when she went down—for she had spent a pleasant morning amongst the youngsters, and she anticipated a most pleasant evening—her bright face clouded when she found "not there" the rector's nephew, Harry Anderson, for nearly three months had elapsed since last she saw him. His friends at Oxford would not part with him—so he said at the station where he met his cousin—as there were lots of parties on hand for a week or more.

Now he and Nelly were but mere acquaintances, and had only known each other for some eighteen months; but the non-fulfilment of the hopes raised by the rector on the previous evening had an effect on her; and notwithstanding that the party was a very merry one, it was not without an effort on her own part that she was able to make a show of enjoying herself; for, though Harry knew it not, he was with Nelly an especial favourite; for, as she told her cousin, Annie Hamilton, he was "so nice and gentlemanly, and so kind and clever;" and cleverness with Nelly went a long way, especially cleverness in art, and then he was ten years her senior, and she seemed to look up to him.

"I fear you have tired yourself, Miss Nelly," said Mr. Arundell, "with your kind journeyings amongst the people. Mr. Frank, you really must not let her trot about as she does, and all weathers too; she is our right hand, remember, and if she gets laid up I don't know what we shall do."

But if his sister was subdued, Frank was not; for there was a lady visitor there— Miss Hill, from Leicester—a remarkably fine, showy girl, and a graceful skater, who took his heart by storm, and disturbed him considerably, until, in a month's time from then, he saw in the *Morning Post* the announcement of her marriage to a clergyman. "Oh, hang that curate!" Frank said, when he saw it. "The Church has claims, we know; but— well, confound it! a plainer girl would do to district visit." So Nelly laughed, and plagued him ever after, and quoted his own words to him when, as was the case some time afterwards, it became evident to her that there was a chance of the rector's daughter, pretty Clara Arundell, becoming her sister-in-law.

Friend Freeman too got hit—a London lady equally good looking—but to no purpose, for before he had forgotten her, he heard she had eloped, and with a doctor.

As they had all been up late the night before, the party at the rectory broke up early; and Frank and Nelly were on their way home by ten o'clock. Just as they reached the end of the Church-lane, to turn up the avenue, they heard some footfalls crunching on the snow, and turning, stopped. It was Burt the doctor, who pulling up, shook hands with each of them.

"The very man," said he. "Lawson of Landimoor is very ill. I am just come from there. They sent for me this morning, and I went; but I found him then in such a queer form, I thought it well to ride round in the evening." "What is it?" Frank said. "On the drink again?" "Well, yes, I fancy so; but I can tell you more about him in the morning; I shall be round early. We must

not keep you in the cold, Miss Hamilton."
"We will go down there at once and see
him, Nell; it is not late." "I think to-night
he had better be kept quiet; say in the
morning, after I have seen him. He may
be better then. I have given him a good
stiff dose of henbane to steady his nerves,"
said the doctor, "and shall continue it. But
I will ride up through the wood in the
morning to see your father, and I daresay by
then I shall be able to tell you more about
him. So now good-night, your sister will
take cold. Good-night, Miss Hamilton."
"Good-night then, doctor. A cold and dreary
ride you'll have to Upperton." "May be so,
Hamilton, all one to me. By day and night
at each one's beck and call, we neither think
of time nor heed the weather. We are like
you hunting men; for what we have to do
we go and do it. See, there's a fox just
making off from Gilbert's for the cover. Good-

night, I'll hasten him." And off the doctor
went and Tally O'd him.

"Well Nell," said her father, as they came
up to the lawn gate, "you are back in good
time. You spied me, Frank, before I saw
you, by 'the view' you gave, though I was
looking for you." "It was no 'Tally O'
of mine, governor; it was the doctor." "What,
Burt?" "Yes, he viewed a fox as he left us,
so could not help opening. He had been to
Landimoor—George Lawson's ill." "The
deuce he is! that's drink." "Something like
it, I expect. I told you he was getting on
last night." "Aye, I hope he will drop it
though, if he wants to remain my tenant.
We must have a look down there in the
morning and give him a hint, if we can, to be
steady." "Yes, we will, but the doctor said
we had better wait till he saw us. He will
ride up here after he has seen him." "Oh,

very well. I have seen to the stables, Frank,
it is all right there; so let us come in now
and get to bed." "The stars are keen."
"Yes, they are; no hunting yet, my lad."

CHAPTER V.

LAWSON OF LANDIMOOR.—A FATHER'S CURSE.

"Good morning," said Frank, as he met the men on the morrow as they came to work, those by the hop-yards below Landimoor. "Do you know how Lawson is?" "In a rummish sort o' a waay, a reckun, meyster," said Roberts, "fur a wan a cussin a good un as we comed boy now jist." "Is, a wan a gwain it sure-ly," said Potts. "He had better let the governor catch him cursing," said Frank, "he will put it on to him." "Somebody's eyes an lims wan a havin it, that's sure," said Turner, "but it wan rayther too hot o' the pepper fur we chaps, it wan, so we slink-ed boy loike, us did, and comed on up thun 'ood." "Is his son at home, young George?" "A reckon a be, sur," said Potts, "as the doctor teld em a munna be laft; a wan ooth him, sur, laaitish last noight." "Yes I know he was, for I met him," said Frank. "Potts you shall help William this morning I want Benbow to go to town for us, so he must catch old Noah. You can see to these draining tiles, Turner; and Roberts, I have told Shepherd he shall have you for a butty, as we want those places squared up quickly, for if the frost goes there will be no time for it, for we must get on the land."

"Bin them ghosties," said Roberts, " alleys o' one colour, meyster, whoite uns?"

"Ghosts," said Frank; "why what have you seen one?"

"No a hanna sur, but oud Tom Baaylis ool ha' it as he did, but it wan a black un."

"When was that?" "New Year's Eve, sur, an a she un, all in black, as comed across the road an oover the stoile loike fur the dingle. But theer" said Roberts, "oud Tom had bin hevin a bout at the cy-der shop, an a wan a troyin to maake his legs carry his body, but as a couldna be claire in his yud a teld him it wan a dawg." "What did he say?" "'Dawg,' says a, 'thin it wan a dawg in petticuts, an foive foot ten.'" "Well," laughed Frank, "I certainly never heard of a black ghost, those who believe in them always say they are white." "Now does 'em, sur, sure?" said Roberts. "Well that be a comfort, a mortal sort o' comfort, sure-ly, fur a dunna loike to hear o' them things bein about nohow. It souns horful loike, an terrifyin anz ockard for we chaps, as han to be through them dingles laaitish. Marnins dunna matter, so as the cocks ha' croud. They alleys hucks it when them cocks be crouing, they does."

"Well," said Frank, "as they have now been crowing for some time, I think you, too, had better 'hook' it, and get on to work, for here are the women I see coming, and not a blow struck yet. I think, when you and Shepherd come to that bit at the corner, where it's all down, you'll want a stake or two; but you'll see. Keep them low if you do use them, for they are nasty things for horses." "We 'ool, meyster. Shepherd an' me 'll see aboot it, sur."

"Well, you women, it's cold comfort for you," said Frank, as the wives from the common came up. "Go into the back-kitchen and warm you, there is a good fire there." So they went in, and he followed them. "We must hurdle off some of those sheep," said he, "this morning, so get on with the cutting will you, all you can." "Dun yer kneow how Muster Gaarge be this marnin', sur?" asked Mrs. Smith. "Well

got married; but hur oud mother telld ma granmother, an ma granmother telld me, as a 'hoped' it wan roight; but what the letter said as brought the news, was as hur'd 'bettered' aself, ecos that cust oud feyther o' hern had teld hur when hur waanted to come home loike a bit to see 'em, as 'hur'd better stop wheer a wan, till hur'd bettered aself."

"That wan ecos a went awaay agin his will—the oud crab-opple. Now a asks yer, as a Christian woman, Mrs. Gould, an you Sapphira, ef so be as a wan married, right-eously, yer know; righteously, Sapphira, whoy daynt a saay so?" "So a did," interrupted Mrs. Davis, who had always stuck up for her, having known her from a child. "A begs yer pardin, Jemima," said Mrs. Smith, "'bettered aself' wan the words." "But thin daynt a saay," persisted Mrs. Davis, "ef so be as 'm wished to wroite to a, as they wan

to direct the letters, 'Mrs. So-and-so?'"
"In coorse a did; but that wan a bloind fur
the sarvants, that wan, i' them furrin paarts
as a wan agwain to taake hur too. Wheer
wan it, Sapphira?" said Mrs. Smith, "my
memry's bad." "Oh, a dunna kneow," said
Mrs. Pritchett, annoyed at Jane Smith's
obstinacy, "Meriky, or Stralia, or Botternee
Baay, or somewheer."

"Come, now then," said Frank, "make
haste you women and have a warm, and let's
be getting on. What tongues you have!"
"Tom! you young limb—hit him Meyster—
let that theer oud maggit be," said his mother,
as she spied him. "Uz hammer thee nut ef
thee dussent." "Aye," observed Mrs. Smith,
"thee bist alleys a maakin on him imparent,
an a puttin' on him up to saay what he
ossent to we wimmen. Ween wring his neck
ef yer dunna." "Jaaine, Jaaine, pratty
Jaaine—oud Jaaine Smith!" said Peter, sup-

plementing it with "Pritchett, Pritchett, Mother Pritchett. Goo on, goo on, Sapphira," as he caught that individual looking at him—words which caused Tom to vanish, while he had the chance to do so. Mrs. P., however, gave the cage such a vigorous swing as she passed it, that the magpie saw stars immediately, and was in a confused state of maledictions for an hour afterwards; his head remaining on one side, and his claws clutched, showing a praiseworthy attempt on his part to circumvent the enemy, by keeping a good look out, and holding on.

"Frank," cried Nelly, making her appearance at the door in a couple of hours afterwards, "breakfast." And Frank, who had seen to the things and been round the stables, and got all ship-shape for the day, kicked the snow off his boots, came in, and sat down with a good appetite. "Any tidings of Lawson?" said his father. "Not particular," said Frank, "but he can use his voice, I hear, • and Peter's a gentleman to him." "Then he must be bad," said Hamilton. "Bob, unless that bird of yours mends his manners I shall settle him." "He isn't mine, pa; he's Tom's." "Then tell Tom to teach him better." "Papa," said Nelly, "a gentleman on horseback has just come through the gate. Perhaps it is the doctor?" "See, Frank," said his father; and in a few minutes Mr. Burt, looking very rosy from his morning ride, came in, and shook hands with them.

"Well, doctor, and how is the patient this morning?" "Rather better, Hamilton, though still queer." "Then settle down to it, doctor, and make a good breakfast, and you shall tell us all about him afterwards. Mother, a hot plate, please. Now, doctor, don't spare. You must have turned out early?" "I did," said the doctor, buckling

to at the broiled ham and the fried potatoes,
as some fresh hot coffee came in, and Mrs.
Hamilton helped him to it, "though not
out of bed, for I have not been in it."
" No ?" "A case on the down ; so I kicked
my heels there half the night, got back, and
washed, and started. A splendid morning,
keen and crisp; I quite enjoyed it." "Yes,"
said Hamilton, "it is ; but you must have
found it cold, doctor, on that down ?" " You
would have said so had you been there, for
it was on the top of it—Gabriel Jones's
cottage. I counted seven holes in the roof,
where the stars showed through, and the
walls are wattle and dab."

"Parish, of course ?" "Yes." "Note ?"
"Well, I did not stay for it." "No, you
never do. Well, it is a bit for Jemmy."
"So I suppose," said the doctor. "Master
Minchem seldom fails to pull into me when
he has the chance of it. What a screw he

is! Thank you, Mrs. Hamilton; I will take another cup—yes, and a little more ham, Miss Nelly, if I may trouble you. Thank you. They don't cure their hams like this on our side the hill, Mrs. Hamilton. Uncommonly juicy, that it is — thanks, just one spoonful, please. I think fried potatoes are a great institution, Hamilton. I always feel better when I've had them." "Good stayers," was the reply, "so we have them on hunting mornings, as a lining to the waistcoat." "And on all other mornings, too," said his wife, "when we can get you any."

"Well, we are fond of them, that's certain —a Teme-side weakness, eh, mother?" said Frank.

Mr. Burt, of Upperton, called, as is the custom in the country, "Doctor" Burt, was a middle-aged married man, with a large family and a good practice. He was one of the district surgeons—having the care of the four largest parishes of the Union—and also surgeon to the Workhouse, of which he had sole charge; and he was liked by the poor, if not by the Guardians, the interests of the two sometimes clashing; for whether it was meat and arrow-root, or ale or wine that was ordered, though it was always really necessary for the patient, the cost was counted by the "parers" there, and remarks made that meat or wine was "cheap physic for the doctor." Fortunately the Chairman of the Board was a thorough gentleman, and a man of sense, and as there were several others of the Guardians who were quite as considerate as was Mr. Hamilton, in all that related to out-door relief and necessaries for the sick poor, the grinding propensities of the few—the comparatively uncivilised and uneducated ones—rarely brought the doctor much annoyance.

Minchem, of The Hawthorns, who growled

at everything and everybody, was the worst
of them; but as John Hamilton was his
brother-guardian for Eymor ' parish, "oud
Jemmy Pinchem," as the people called him,
generally got the worst of it. "Then you
still go in for risking Jemmy?" laughed
Mr. Hamilton, as they finished breakfast.
"He will oppose you on Board-day, depend
upon it. You will get no fee for last night's
work, that's certain, as you attended without a note." "I will risk that; but I will
tell you what, Hamilton, there is one thing,"
said the doctor, "I am not going to risk for
all the Minchems in creation; and that is,
the lives, or the health, or even the comfort
of a single poor person in my parishes; nor,
if I know it, of man, woman, or child in
the House, so long, at least, as I have the
sole charge of it. The poor have hard lines
enough to encounter, as you know, Hamilton, and I am not going to make things

harder for them when they are down with sickness.

"I have been now Union Surgeon for thirteen years. I always did—it is against the rule I know—and I always will continue to say to them, 'Come for me first, and get the note afterwards—when the Relieving Officer comes round will do, so don't hinder your work to go after it.' It saves their own time, and I can cure them the quicker; and in urgent cases it often saves a life. Still, I grant you, in so doing I have no claim upon you, for, as you know, Hamilton, very clearly, though I am responsible to the Board for my conduct of the case, if I once undertake it, you need not pay me if it is without a note, unless you choose to do so, for you can legally refuse every item. But as I commenced so shall I go on, pay or no pay." "All right," said Mr. Hamilton, amused at the doctor's earnest-

ness, "I'll settle Jemmy for you. Is it an
extra?" "No; ordinary. Merely a tedious
case." "Well, if he disputes the paltry fee
that is all 'my lords' allow, I will tell him
my mind about it, that's certain. Ten shillings!" said Hamilton; "fancy, half the
night on the top of a high hill for it, in
the depth of winter; and—at least humanly
speaking—with a woman's life in your hands
for hours!" "Yes," said the doctor, "and
though we will not for a moment put the
two on the same level, with a good horse
rattling his ribs with the cold, alongside you
—all in the hut together, and not a blanket
to cover him."

"Well, about this tenant of yours, Hamilton. Do you know he is very queer. I
don't half like the look of him. It is not
delirium tremens, though in some respects it
simulates it. It is more like a shock to the
nervous system from great terror. The fellow

seems to be in a continued fright. He is a trifle steadier this morning, as he ought to be, for he has had three teaspoonfuls of henbane in the last twelve hours—in sixty-drop doses—but he is shaky still." "What was it all about," said Hamilton, "what caused it—drink?"

"He had been drinking, his wife said, for he did not get home till late, and then some men brought him—that was the night before last, New Year's Eve, and he was very quarrelsome when he did come home; but as the son was out for the night, they were settling for bed, when it seems the wife made some remark about being careful with the fire, as he wanted to leave it burning; in case his son came home before the morning; and she unfortunately reminded him of that night four years ago, when they were all burnt out at Upperton; the night they heard from Jesse, his daughter. We knew her very well. You and Frank were there, I remember."

"Yes," said Hamilton, "we were. We saw the shine over the woods as we put our candles out and drew the blinds up—we were going to bed—so we dressed at once, and cut away straight across the country, and took the men with us, to see where it was, and to help at it; but, as it was so very far to send for them, the engines were too late; and, as you know, doctor, the place went, and most of the stock with it. It was a sad thing! I did not then know them, but I was sorry in my heart for them; for there the poor fellow sat stupefied in the ruins, gazing at the sickening sight of his four dead horses, each of them roasted to a cinder, and muttering, 'I'm done! I'm done!' and with no roof left to shelter him."

"Well, doctor, Landimoor was vacant then. Jordan, who lived there—he was some re-

lation of theirs by-the-bye—had left it but a
few days before Christmas; so I tapped the
poor chap on the shoulder, and put his
wife's hands into his, and I said, 'Look here,
Mr. Lawson, my name's Hamilton—Hamilton
of Eymor—you may have heard of me.
There is a little place of mine vacant, below
my house; you shall come there till we can
see what can be done in the matter. Make
your mind easy now. I will charge you no
rent for it for six months, or twelve if you like.
So cheer up; my son and I. will get back
at once, and send the rest of the men across
to help you with what's left; and then my
groom, Charles, shall bring you both away
in our covered cart;'—young George, his son,
was away at the time, but he came after.
'By the time you come,' I said, 'we will
have the fires lit, and all made ready for
you; and my girl Nelly shall be there to
make your wife comfortable. Frank and I

will come up again, and see to everything.'
So they both God blessed me; and then,
turning our backs on Applepatch, we left
the still smoking ruins and got back home.

"The next day, or rather some hours afterwards, we had them safe at Landimoor, and
they have remained there. It was a great
come-down for both of them, for it turned
out they were not insured. However I let
them stay there rent-free for the first year,
so as to give them two years to make a
twelvemonth's rent in; and as the son, young
George, is a decent, tidy fellow, and strong
and active, they have pulled along very fairly
since then, as it is a fruity little place, and
money on it."

"It was never known, was it, how the fire
was caused?" "No," said Hamilton; "not
with certainty. That Lewis, who so pestered
the daughter with his attentions before she
left home, was suspected; but without cause,

I should hope, for, loose fellow as he was even then, I cannot think he could have been such a fiend as to fire it." "I don't know," said the doctor, "people will talk; and those about us will have it to this day that he set light to it, and they have shunned him ever since." "Any grounds for it, do you think?" "Well, it seems that he and the old man had words that night, and Lawson turned him out, and told him never to darken his doors again. The fellow was in drink, and he went off swearing, and saying he would be revenged. In less than an hour afterwards my wife heard the cry of 'Fire!' up the village. The rest you know." "Yes," said Hamilton. "What was the quarrel?"

"Something about the daughter who had left home years ago. They had received a letter from her that day, to say she was married and that she was going abroad; or at least that she had 'bettered herself,' which

is the same thing in these parts; and Lawson,
who thought some time or other to marry
her, if she did come home, to a small
farmer in the parish—John Purchas—cursed
her for it, and cursed Lewis as the cause of
it, as it was through him that she left home;
for he had threatened her 'if she would not
have him she should have no one,' and the
girl got afraid of him, as he dogged her about
everywhere. Her home, too, was not comfortable, owing to her father's temper; so
soon afterwards she left Upperton; but where
she went was kept a secret, that Lewis might
not annoy her." "Where was the girl then,
for they have never heard from her?"

"I don't know, nor could her father remember; for on reading the letter he crunched it
it up and flung it in the fire; and the loss
of his stock and things that same evening
was such a shock to him that he could not
afterwards remember place or number, more

than it was somewhere in London for a' week or two, if they wished to see her at home or there, and then abroad; but where it was he could not call to mind; for, as I said, he burnt the letter in his passion as soon as he had read it. So no reply could be sent to her." "They have never heard again from her, then? I have not myself liked to press them about it," said Hamilton, "as I could see they did not care to speak of her." "I don't think they have," said the doctor; "I should say not, as the wife told me that for nearly twelve months before they heard from her her father had ceased to write to her, and would not let her do so; and that he had, in fact, had words with her and his son several times because they persisted in replying to her. So it seems as they did not write to her she ceased to write to them, and no doubt she was strengthened in that determination by a brutal message—or rather letter,

for he himself wrote it—that she had pre-
viously received from him, in reply to her
own letter, in which she wished to come home
to see them all for a week or two."

"What sort of a girl was she?" "Oh, a
high-spirited, fine-grown girl, and not bad
looking; and about eighteen or twenty, I
should say, when she left Upperton. I think,
in the first instance, she went as nursery-
governess to a lady friend of the rector's,
somewhere near London, and then elsewhere;
but I am not sure. I only know she has
never been seen since then by any one in
our neighbourhood, unless it was that Lewis,
who, they do say, tracked and bothered her;
and that must now be nine or ten years ago
—quite that." "Was she a tidy girl? No
reason for thinking she went wrong, was
there?" "I should say not, for she had
the name of being a quiet, decent girl, and
I always thought her sedate and steady; and

up to the time of her writing home she was in some situation. But although I have often heard the matter talked of, I really know but very little of it beyond mere village gossip."

" Just so," said Hamilton."

" Well, as to Lawson, doctor: you were saying that he seems to have a fright on him. What makes you think so?" "What the wife told me. When the talk began about the fire, it put him out sadly, and he commenced to rave about his daughter as the cause of it, and the cause also of all his ill luck, as ever since she married, things, he said, had gone wrong with him; and the more his wife tried to stop him, the worse he went on, till at last he fell to and cursed Jesse stoutly, and continued to curse her. It was in vain Mrs. Lawson tried to pacify him, as he was in drink and dogged; and while she had her arms round him, crying her eyes out, poor woman, to think a father

should so curse his daughter, she saw his
eyes staring like a statue, and then she said
he gave a scream, more like a woman than
a man, and fell down stiff. She got him
up to bed when he came round, but, her
son being out and no one there to help her,
he lay there in his clothes for hours, con-
vulsed and shuddering, with both his hands
pressed close against his face; and all she
could get out of him was, 'that white face
at the window! 'twas hers; she heard me!'"

"How very odd," said Hamilton. "Of
course 'twas fancy?" "Purely imaginary,
a prick of conscience. He had been off on
the drink, and hence the fancy. He is
steadier now, but still that 'white face'
haunts him, and every now and then he
cowers beneath the bed-clothes out of sight."
"I think you said 'twas not delirium tremens?" "No, though very like it. Unless
he mends, though, soon, his brain will turn.

Fancy or not, the shock to him is great. His son is with him; but unless to-night I find that he is calmer, perhaps you would let your wagoner sit up along with him, to help the son in case of sudden dash?" "I will," said Hamilton. "You'll do your best by him, I know; I'll see you paid." "Don't name it," said the doctor. "He shall not want for help. To-night I'll see him; but now I must get on, for lots are waiting, and to-day my round's a long one." "Well, I won't detain you, doctor. Joe, the horse," cried Mr. Hamilton, as they went out. "Why, how his coat stares, doctor!" "Yes, so would yours, had you been where he was. Good-bye till evening." "Good-bye," said Hamilton.

CHAPTER VI.

A WINTER NIGHT.——A WHITE FACE AT THE WINDOW.

THAT white face at the window was no fancy. When, through the unsteadiness of his legs, Tom Baylis fell down in the road on the night of New Year's Eve, the "ghost" that went by him, and that contributed so much to sober him, was none other than a woman in dark clothes, who had been for a considerable time sheltering from the snow in the cart-shed by the road; and who seemed, from the stealthy way in which, since the snow had ceased, she had kept creeping out and looking up the road, as if she were anxious to escape notice.

Seeing that there was no one else in sight when the old fellow fell down, she left her hiding-place, and hurrying across the bridge, got over the stile beside it, and ran up the hop-yard for some distance; then hid again behind one of the piles of poles that were stacked there.

Listening and screening her eyes, the better to make out the bearings of the white world around her, she presently went on along the hop-yard from one pile to another, until she got to the meadow beyond it, which she crossed rapidly, and reached the stile which separated it from the dingle. Getting over it, she crept from the footpath into the bushes, and again listened; but the tolling of the church bells for the closing of the year, being the only sound she heard, she came out again to the path, and drawing a warm shawl that was underneath her cloak closer round her, rested against the stile.

While there, the sound of noisy voices to the left of her made her shrink back again into the bushes, and keep closely within the shadows of the trees; as here and there, as the moon was rising, light crossed the path. At last, when the sound of voices had almost ceased, and then had come back to her louder than ever, until it wholly ceased—people returning to the village by the foot-road from Landimoor—she hurried along the path, and dipping down into the deep shadow of the dingle, reached the foot-bridge there that crossed the brook; and brushing the snow off a rough seat that was near it, sat down and remained there, seemingly in deep thought.

Suddenly—for the sound of a voice came to her—she jumped up, and bending forwards in a listening attitude, put her hand to her heart and dropped upon the bench again; where, burying her face in her hands and tapping with her foot, she continued to sway backwards and forwards, while her tears fell fast; for the voice, the voice of one "in drink," she knew, though many years had passed since last she heard it.

Jumping up again as the sound faded from her, she hastened along the winding path, pressing back the bushes as she went, until, crossing another foot-bridge — for the brook wound about there — she saw before her a wider pathway, and between the trees a small farm-house and buildings in a clearing. It was Landimoor—a cousin of her's had lived there years ago, and so she knew it; as she used, when quite a school-girl, to come and see him there—him and his sister, Henrietta Jordan. But as she hurried up between the trees, a door slammed-to beyond, and then she stopped, as if she were undecided, and had another cry, and sat there some time on some fallen timber.

At length, getting up hastily, as though she had made her mind up, she went straight for the building, to where there was a light visible; rested for a moment against the hayrick, stepped noiselessly through the wood-yard, passed the hovel at the end of it, and turning round the corner, reached the back of the house.

Putting her hand on the wicket that led into the garden, she paused; came back, went again, and listened; and then creeping silently to the side window, stepped on to the ledge beneath it, and lifting herself by the sill, looked in.

But she had no sooner done so, than she dropped from the window, and staggered back against the shed, with "No hope, no hope! may God in Heaven help me!" as the sound of a man's voice was heard inside the house, raving and cursing.

Dashing the tears from her eyes, she again went to the window; and raising herself up, flattened her face against it as his passion increased, and sobbingly implored him not to curse her! But the storm of his own voice, and the continued hooting of the owls in the trees there, drowned the sound; and her piteous cry of " Oh, father, father! don't you curse me so! " went away on the wind.

" Curse her! " roared Lawson, " curse her, I say—curse her for ever, the jade; may she never darken my doors again! " and dropping from the window as his eyes seemed to glare at hers as if he really saw her, she heard a scream as she did so, and answering it instinctively with " Mother! mother! " she rushed to the wicket to get into the house. The gate was locked, and so resisted all her frantic efforts. She fell back by it on the snow, and fainted.

And as the sweet sound of the church bells—now pealing joyously—came up from the valley, she, who years ago left home a happy girl, lay there heart-broken; homeless and helpless—almost penniless; her last hope gone! her father's roof denied her.

Merrily chime the bells, and merrily sing the ringers, "Peace and good-will, peace and good-will, peace and good-will for the year that is in."

"Now lads," says Abraham Peplow to his mates, as they each stand rope in hand on the lower floor of Eymor belfry, "with a will, plase, ta sind a good sound inta iviry art as hears us. Bin yer ready?" "Roight," said Burton the blacksmith, who answered for the rest of them. Down come the ropes, and up go the bells; and the musical peal of six, as they vary the swing of it, echoes to the hills.

"What bin the toime now, Bill?" said Turner, as they finished it. "Early it," said Burton, "it inna half arter." "A shoon a thought it weer welly noigh wun!" "Not loikely, Potts," said Roberts. "Whoy yer baynt fur bed too, it, bin yer?" said Byfield. "Ween han harf-a-dozen peals it afore ween done ooth 'em." "That's right; bother time," said Walker, "let the bells be done justice to. I've been clerk now a matter of twenty years, and I don't think we've finished any year before two. Go on, Abraham, the master won't mind it."

"How long 'ool the drink last," said Peplow. "O, iver so long," said Isaac. "Depinds how we han it," said Potts, who was a thirsty one; "ef koind loike, it 'ool be out soonish." "Look you here," said the clerk, "here are seven of us. If Abraham's agreeable, I'll be a matter of a shillin' to your sixpences, there now! just for the sake o' the bells, and harmony." "Whatn yer saay, maites?" said Peplow. "Agreed," they said, and each put down his sixpence. "Good," said Isaac, as he added a shilling to them. "Now, I call that acting like men; we shall be right now for an hour or two; so I propose we finish what's left, at once, and then two of you chaps can take the cans to the shop to be filled again."

"Oon yer han, cy-der or yale?" said Potts, who, with Burton, proposed fetching it. "Cy-der," said Abraham, "it oona do ta be a mixin on it, whoile we bin hot a pullin; let it be cy-der, an then ween goo home steady an paceable, as becomes us, as ringers." "But we baynt a gwain home it," urged Potts, who wanted to mix it a bit, "an the yale's goodish; maake it yale now, an cy-der arterwards." "A oona ha' it," said Peplow; "a said cy-der an a manes it, an uz head ringer." "Roight," said Roberts, "we defers to you Abram, we mun begin the New Year well, or the parson ool be on ta us." "Now pour out an drink," said Peplow, "let it be cy-der." "The clerk fust, maaites." "And you next, as head ringer," said Walker, handing it. "Fill it hup," said Burton, as his turn came, "a full horn or nerrun. Happy New Year to yer all, an maay it bring some peals."

"Ha kneow whoon be fur the fust call," said Byfield. "Muster Eddutt." "Han a gid the order?" said Potts. "No a hanna," said Abraham. "Not loikely it, hany ways. No, heen waaite till the flowers bin out. Primeroses moight do, they moight, if they wan ony out; but snowdrops bin nohow, theym orful onlucky, as yer moight kneow if sa be as yer gid a thought ta it. Would theer be a gull i' the plaice now if yer broughten in, a shoon loike to kneow? Answer ma that neow. In coorse theer oodna; an boy the saame token, if snowdrops bin strewed theyn ha' no youngsters. So maike yer moinds asy neow o' that lot, cos theer mun be youngsters, fur theer's money to lave; consickavently they oona be married till the flowers be come."

"Hur's rayther a nate un," said Byfield, alluding to Miss Wood, the bride elect of Edward Warrilow, " a killed a pig fur they isterday—a noice baacon un o' sixteen scoore, an a looked hur hover. A calls hur pratty."
"An so hur be," said Burton, "a shoes hur pony—Lard love him, aint the oud mon heavy though. A shouldna oonder now ef a wanna worth a thousan' pound amost." "A thousand!" said the clerk, "aye, ten of 'em. A very saving sort of man is Jabez." "Lard bless us an saave us, but yer dunna manc it, Isaac?" "But I do," said Walker. "An when bin the laaidies at oud Jemmy's agwain to gie us a turn, Tom?" asked Roberts. "A dunna kneow," said Potts, whose daughter lived there. "God bless the mon as has em, saay I,

they bin all tarred wi' the saame brush, theer. Oud Jemmy's a cust un, and so bin they, both cust uns.   Our Liza says they be a naggin an a caggin at it all daay long, an be niver satisfoied.   A manes to lave 'em if so be as they dunna alter.   A ony wish ud got Jaane's plaace at Muster John's.   That bin a plaace if you loike, that be."

"Is," said the pig killer after due reflection, so as to speak decisively, "good uns all." "That's sure," said the blacksmith, "theer's a good missis ef yer loike, an a meyster.   Aye an a young meyster too.   An as fur the young missus,—well, ood shoe hur pony fur nothin ! theer now, that a ood; darn ma body if a oodna.   Hur's alleys a smoile fur a feller hur has, an somethin' civil too to saay t'un, an so han the tothers.   They bin all good uns, most alarmin' good uns, that they bin," said he emphatically.   "Yes," said the clerk, "I wish we had more of the same sort; they are

often at the rectory. Our master's partial
to em."

"Can's out, boys. Who's fur the shop?"
"Hand it over, Abram; me an Bill ool fatch
it." So Potts and Burton started. "If old
George Lawson's there still, tell him to come
up," said Walker. "A ool," said Potts. But
when they returned with the cider they said
he had been gone long ago, for as he was
getting on a bit and inclined to be trouble-
some, Amphlett "swored as he oodna draw
him not no more;" so at that some o' the
chaps "as wan theer tooked him ome, an left
him a cussin comfortably."

"The oud 'ooman ool have a baddish
toime on it to-night, a reckon, fur young
Gaarge bin out," said Burton; "a bin got
orful waspish bin the oud mon laately; can-
tankerous loike an woild." "Putt the cans
i' the corner, Bill, and kiver 'em oover, an
thin ween tackle 'em when ween had a peal.

Dooty fust, maaites, an' the tipple arter. Now thin, all hands to the ropes!" And again the joy-bells rang right merrily.

And the poor half-dazed girl in the snow —who had raised herself on one arm—was trying, with her head dropped on to the other, to make out what it all meant; that surging, and swaying, and ceasing of sound, as the wind took it and sent it. But she could make nothing of it—nothing distinct at least—only a glimmering, as it were, of some great happiness to her, herself; and, as they "fell" the bells, of some great grief; a loss that took not shape, and well it was for her it did not do so.

But linked with both there was a void, a blank, a seeming sense of utter loneliness— the numbing influence of the cold night-air, the ceasing of the sound. And over all that blotted all else out, some sudden, cruel, and unlooked-for blow, that sent a rush—

oppression—to her heart, and brought a dread, a weighty sense of evil happening, and made her start, and press both hands quite tightly to her brow, to think it out!

But all in vain; cold stupefies, and slowly dulls the brain, inducing sleep—sleep that too often knows no more a waking. The effort only brought her fear and terror; some savage curse that seemed to crush her down; escape from something, and from somebody; an inability to get away; a dim bewildering sense to try to hide—a sense that saved her dying in the snow, there at her father's door —for, creeping on into the shed, she crouched there, down in a corner into heaped-up straw; and then she slept, soundly and heavily.

Safe from the wind, and warm, too, where she was, the icy bond that held her brain was broken. With warmth came circulation, and then sense; and when she woke, she woke to realise both where she was and what

she had to face. It came back bit by bit,
though indistinctly; but still she felt that
she must "see" her mother—and see ‑him.

The sky had clouded over, snow was falling; no light, no sound; the ticking of the
clock was all she heard, and strong hard
breathing; and as she dare not rouse them,
there she stayed, to wait till daylight,—for a
home or none,—and, buried in the straw, she
slept again.

It was but troubled sleep, though, brief
and fitful; her own dreams frightened her;
and as the clock struck four she woke again,
woke with a gulp and sob, to dry the tears
that trickled down her cheeks, and know
her father's curse was no mere dream. She
seemed to see those words in all their black-
ness; they seemed writ there as she looked
on the snow; that "curse her, curse her!"
burnt into her brain; she felt its crushing
weight upon her heart, felt that a little

more would drive her mad;—as she had felt before, when troubles came.

The snow fell fast; the owls kept hooting at her; she could not drive her own thoughts back again. The wind, each creak, each rustle made her start; the very straightening of the straw caused terror ; until, unable to keep crouched down there, she rushed out of the shed into the snow, and tried the gate again ; and then another, that she found as she wandered round about. Both locked ! No chance but waiting.

Wait ? Not in the shed again, for rats were there; she thought their breath had been against her face, she knew she felt them pass across her feet. Not by the house ; her father's curse seemed there—he might come out and curse her where she stood. Out in the open till her mother came—her own dear mother, who was always kind— aye, out in the open, in the driving snow;

it would hide her from the owls, who did but mock her. Out there, out anywhere, so that she was not still. And down the bank she went, with but one purpose—to move about, and try to drive back thought.

She wandered listlessly, as chance directed, now through the bushes, then on open ground; again through bushes, then between tall trees; and still the snow came down, and in such flakes that all around was very nearly hidden. She turned back twice, but could not find her way; she tried again, she still was in a wood; she called—no answer—and rushed madly on, to find her home—her home that was denied her.

Hope came; she reached the brook. Yes, all was right. Her foolish fears were simply foolish fancies. She soon should reach the house, and then—would wait. Yes, there was Eymor brook, the brook she crossed; but where she crossed it was a mile away!

past the steep wood, beyond the long green valley, down in the dingle where she heard the owls. She had wandered on from Landimoor and lost her way.

She kept the water's edge—a high fence stopped her; she tried the other way—a fence again. She could scarcely see for snow, but still went on—all trees and briars; another try—all rails. She hit the brook again; there was no way out; and unless help came, she must sink down and die— die in the snow, and perhaps in sight of home!

Nerved at the thought, she found the hedge again, and, with a frantic effort, then crushed through it, and dropped into a meadow down below; when, creeping up a bank, she reached the road; but where she was she knew not, nor did she know which way to turn, or where she ought to go. She seemed bewildered. She felt fast sinking, and could go no further, and thought her home must now be miles away. It was not one mile, but she had kept on walking.

The snow came faster, and despair came with it, for her father's curse kept ringing in her ears, · and made her once more feel that wish to hide, to get away, to rush on anywhere away from him.

Stumbling along, half blinded by the snow, she heard the rush of water—the weir at the mill, for she was near it—a dangerous sound to her at such a moment, poor helpless girl! It seemed to tell of all her troubles over, of peace and rest; and, with a cry, she rushed on to the river.

When daylight came, her footsteps were all covered; no trace was left of Jesse in the snow.

CHAPTER VII.

ARNOLD JACKSON—THREE TO ONE.

In alluding to the subdued manner of Nelly Hamilton at the rector's party, and to the probable cause thereof, we remarked that her acquaintance with Harry Anderson had been but of short duration, and that nearly three months had elapsed since she had seen him.

How they became known to each other we will shortly state, as we shall have to know more about them as our narrative proceeds. But we will first speak of him and the rector's family, and of his connection with them.

"Harry" Anderson—so named—was the only child of the rector's brother-in-law, George Anderson, the well-known artist of Fitzroy Square, whose pictures still attract attention and command high prices at Christie's. Losing his wife soon after he became a Royal Academician, George Anderson decided to carry out her earnest wishes that their only child, a smart lad of fourteen, who was then at Eton, should be allowed to follow his own inclinations in being brought up to his father's profession instead of to the Church.

At the age, therefore, of seventeen he left Eton and came home, where he was at once placed in the studio; where, working hard at the flat and the round, under his father's guidance, he was soon well grounded in the rudiments of art, and light and shade; and after three years of careful plodding and judicious study, his father's care was well rewarded by the symptoms of undoubted talent that the lad possessed.

Advanced, in his twentieth year, from oils and mill-board for studies, to the dignity of oils and canvas for pictures, Harry Anderson exchanged for the greater part of the year the confinement of the studio for the health and freedom of the open air; where, face to face with Nature day by day, he soon corrected the inevitable mannerisms of the studio, and exchanged for rustic truth the set pose of the draped model; and the painty look that had hitherto been more or less apparent in all his work, was soon lost in his loosened foliage, his freer touch, and a closer observation of those gradations of tone that, nowhere so well acquired as in the open, are indispensable to the production of a truthful picture.

Quick to recognise colour and to see form— as the breadth and fulness between his eyes clearly testified—he had acquired by the end of his first out-door year a familiarity with foreground detail, and a good knowledge of gradational distance. The next year his improvement was still greater, as, giving more time to his pictures, he painted fewer of them; and he had now obtained a pulpy touch, move, and atmosphere; and his skies, that were no longer patterned, showed varying effects, that were carefully reflected on the landscape under. It was a good year's work. Before the end of his third year of out-door work he had made such a stride in tone and tint and general effect in truth to nature, that, tired of seeing his pictures piled against the wall or hung only in the studio, he begged to be allowed to paint a picture for exhibition; but his father, to whom nothing short of real excellence was sufficient, refused at present to allow him to do so.

Wearied, however, by the lad's pertinacity,

and by his confidence in his own powers, he
—as it might also perhaps save his own
pocket—at length met him half-way, by con-
senting to his selling, if he could do so, his
pictures to a dealer, provided such pictures
had not his name to them.

"Pot‑boilers" in one sense, though not
in another — for they were by no means
"scamped" pictures — he, on his own re-
sources, tried first one man and then another,
until, tired of letting what was really good
honest work go month after month for a
mere trifle—just a pound or two, the rascally
crew grinding him down to the lowest shilling, while they were selling his works, small
and unframed as they were, for five, or six,
or seven pounds apiece, for they themselves
took good care to sign his name to them, his
father's name being well known—he wearied
of the whole thing and decided to shut it
up altogether; and to wait, as he had been

advised to do, until he could place on the walls of one or other of the Exhibitions such a picture that even his father should consider not only worth showing, but worth having. Accident, however, befriended him, and he soon slid into the right groove.

At this time he was a smart, good-looking young fellow of three-and-twenty, tall, lithe, and active; with firmness in his muscles, and a healthy colour in his face, from his outdoor employment.

Returning one evening from the Garrick Club, where he had been spending an hour or two with an artist friend—it was in the summer—he saw before him, as he crossed on his way home, from King Street to Cranbourne Street, the figure of a young girl crouching in a doorway, and picking up flowers that were scattered there. She moved as he approached, and then ran off rapidly, as three young fellows, who were on the opposite side, ran after her and chased her into a court just beyond there. As he came up to the place—Earl's Court—he heard high words, and the sound of a girl crying; and though such sounds in that neighbourhood were then almost as common as when it was Cranbourne Alley, curiosity, or rather manliness, induced him to stand a moment, and he soon heard sufficient to make him enter the court to go up to them; and as he did so, the three who had followed the girl, were making a rush at a young fellow who was there, and who seemed to be about seven or eight-and-twenty, behind whom the girl stood crying, and shrinking in a doorway.

"Now, look here," said he, as he kept them off and screened her, " You confounded, cowardly beggars, though you are three to one, if you don't let the girl alone, and be off about your business, it will be the worse for you. I don't want a row, and I won't have one if I can help it; but, mark me, the first who lays a hand on her to pull her about, I'll floor. Stand back, you vagabond," said he, as one of them advanced, " or I'll put a mark on you."

"What's all this about?" said Harry Anderson, pushing his way through the crowd that was collecting—the prospect of a row in that neighbourhood being always attractive—and who were picking up some of the flowers that were strewn about there.

"What's that to do with you?" said the tallest of them. "This," said he, "that as it seems to me you are insulting that girl, you will not touch her while I am here." "But we'll touch you, if you interfere with us." "Will you? Hold my stick, my good girl," said Anderson, as he got round to the one who was by her, and passed it behind him, "and keep where you are. I have not the pleasure of knowing this gentleman," he

said to them, "but it is three to one, and
that is enough for me; so I shall aid him
in protecting this girl, whoever she is. Now,
stand back!"

"Thanks," said the stranger, "you are a
good fellow; but don't let me draw you into
a row. These swells here have been running
her—she is one of the flower-girls—down
Long Acre, and have kicked her basket over
twice, and pulled her about, till they have
frightened her out of her life almost—never
mind, my girl, we'll make it right for you—
and they will either let her alone, or take
the consequences." "Right," said Harry,
"now, look here, you three; give the girl
a crown between you, for the loss of her
flowers, and then clear out, that she may
go her way." "Clear out?" "Yes, clear
out; for if you don't you'll have to take a
licking." "Clear out yourself, you cur,"
cried the taller one. "Cur, eh?—keep still

girl; don't stir till we've settled them—that for you then!" said Anderson, and with a well-directed blow the spokesman of the party was sent against the shutters; his companion who was next to him rapping them, almost simultaneously, from the same cause—a right and left—just as the other one was knocked off his legs by a thud from the girl's protector.

For ten minutes blows were exchanged freely, as they went at it hard and fast— for the fellows could use their fists though they were screwed—when the crowd, wishing to have a share in it, hustled them up the court, and kicked them out of it, a policeman making his appearance as they did so. A few words of explanation ensued, when the kicked ones were told by the policeman that if they did not at once walk off, he would run them in.

"Who is it they've been puttin' on?" said

Robert. "One of the flower-girls. Where do you live?" said Anderson, as he bent down to her. "In Drury Lane, please sir." "Well, don't cry, my girl. Here," said he, as he gave her a couple of half-crowns, "will that put you right for the flowers?" "Oh yes, sir, thank you, sir, and more than their worth too," said the girl, getting up and bobbing a curtsey, and then bursting out afresh, "Oh, sir, you are good; oh dear, dear me, but I can't help crying, sir; you are good, you are."

"Hillo! Jenny; what, have they been mislesting of you?" said Robert, turning the official bull's-eye on to her. "I thought I knew the sound o' your voice anyhow." "She's a decent girl, sir," said that individual confidentially. "It's little Jane Jinniver, of Crown Court; she always makes a bit of a move when I tells her to. I'm obligated to move 'em on, you know sir, and she's never imperent nor saucy. She's not a bad sort, sir, take my word for it; she helps to keep her mother, poor ooman, who's down with the rheumatics. A cousin o' mine, his missis and him, lives nigh 'em." "Oh, well, your beat lies here it seems?" "To the top o' the Acre, sir, and I'll see her safe. Come along, Jen, those swells be gone. I'd ha' locked 'em up if they hadn't four-wheeled it quickish." "And you'll tell mother, will you then, in the morning, how I got it?" said the girl, alluding to the five shillings, for she'd know the button-holes couldn't ha' made it, and I don't want her to be a thinkin' badly of me. You'll do that, won't you?" "I'll tell her, I'll square that, Jen; trust to me for that. Come along, lass. She is but seventeen, sir," said he, stepping back a bit, "but her's very tidy; although" continued he, lowering his voice to a confidential tone, "her sister's gone to the bad, and is doin' penal. She were a bad un, she were, and no mistake, though started tidy and in good service, sir. Oh, yes, Miss Emma's a neat un, she is, sir. Been up and down to everythin, from child stealin up'ards."

" Child stealing ! " said the stranger, " no matter, then, what becomes of her, the wretch! I lost a little sister once myself." "Did you, sir ? " said Robert, " aye, there's a good many as loses 'em now-a-days ; they strips 'em, then turns 'em up, and leaves 'em." " Well, see to this girl, then, will you, and put that in your pocket for your trouble ; " and pocketing the two-shilling-piece given him, the worthy Robert went on and joined the girl, who, with a profusion of thanks to them for their kindness, repaid them by the sight of her now smiling face, for the little scrimmage, they had had for her.

" Now, then," said Harry, as he knocked the dust off him, " which way do you steer ?

My name's Anderson." "And mine's Jackson. Oh, where you like. Let us go across to Smith's at the corner, and get a tidying." So they went.

"I wish the lookers-on had not made a rush at them as they did," said Jackson, as they sat at supper, "for I had just got my man's head in chancery, and I could have done him justice; for I think I could have held him there till I had polished off the other one." "I saw you doing double duty," said Anderson; "but mine was obstinate, and took more licking than I thought he would, or I should have relieved you. I only wish my friend Edmonds had been with me; we could have had a nice little mill then, one and one, but we parted at the Garrick. He is a dab hand with his fists, is Master Herbert, and plucky." "Not Edmonds, the artist?" "Yes, a very good fellow, but he exhibits as 'Herbert.'" "I know he does." "Do you know him, then?" "Well, only this," laughed Jackson, "that he is about my most intimate friend, and my father buys his pictures." "Then you——" "Are Arnold Jackson, the son of James Jackson, the picture-dealer." "And I," said Harry, "am Harry Anderson, the son of the R.A. of that name, and painting 'pot-boilers' for ready-money."

"Well met," said Jackson, "artists all. Let's grip your hand. Now," said he, as he finished his supper, "one good turn deserves another. What can I do for you? Anything in my line?" "Yes," said Anderson, striking while the iron was hot, "get your father to look at my pictures ; for, though I have seen most of the others, I have not been to him "—but he did not say because, in artist circles, James Jackson was known as " Old Jemmy, the screw." " I will," said Jackson. " What are your subjects ? " " Landscapes chiefly, and rustic figures." " The first a drug, and the latter must be good. Anyway father shall see them, and I'll stick them into him if I can." " You are very good," said Anderson. " Will you come across to our place to-morrow and see them, and let me introduce you to my governor ? You could fix then on those you think the likeliest. You might know the studio—the corner house in Fitzroy Square ? " " The old man does, but I don't. What time ? " " Say twelve." " I'll do so; and then you can come back with me to Bond Street." " Agreed ; so now I'll make a move, or I shall miss my train," said Harry Anderson.

" What line is yours ? " " The main one from Victoria, the 12.15, and out at Brixton. I shall barely catch it. Our place is at Tulse Hill." " And my train too, to Herne Hill.

We are at Dulwich." . "Just right then. So
now come on and let us cab it quickly."
"Here you are, sir!—four-wheeler?" "No,
hansom. Now, cabby, quick!—the 12.15
Victoria, and don't you miss it." But cabby,
who had his eye-teeth about him, and knew
it was the last train—to suit their purposes—
did miss it; "ony by harf a minite though,"
said he, as the train steamed out of the
station; so they dismissed him. But as the
fellow pleaded very hard for the journey—
"it'll just about make up my bit o' money,
gentlemen, and times be ockard"—they
jumped in again.

"Denmark Hill and Red Post Road, I
suppose, sir?" "No," said Jackson; "bear
to the right at Vauxhall bridge, and over
Stockwell Green. My friend's for Tulse Hill,
and I beyond the 'Greyhound.'" "All right,
sir. Turn at the church, set down at Water
Lane, and on to Dulwich." "Right you are.

Here, cabby, have a smoke." So cabby took
the weed and drove them quickly.

"Then you have only one sister living?"
said Harry, as they compared notes as they
bowled along the road. "No, only one, and
she is married. They live at Streatham—
John Armiger. His place is in the City—
Welch and Armiger. I say but one; God
knows if Polly's living. Poor girl, we lost
her!"

"How very sad! I heard you say that
you had lost a sister. And what age was
she?" "Oh, ten, within a month. A
pretty child, a merry little puss. She was
my pet; we used to romp together. That's
just six years ago this very summer. It
broke my mother's heart, and nearly mine.
She has never been the same since then,
nor I, nor father." "A grown-up girl, then,
now, if she be living?" "Yes, just sixteen.
God help her if she is! It makes me look

at each young girl I meet, well-dressed or ragged. It's horrid, dreadful, such uncertainty ! "

"The servant-girl we had turned out a thief, and so we sacked her; and she—the wretch, the demon !—took the child, and I think sold her. The only trace we had was through some gipsies. From one chance word we feared she was with their tribe, then camped in Surrey ; but though I routed every tent for miles—have since, do now—we never, spite of all the means we tried, heard more of her. We lived at Matlock then : we left there and came here for better chance. She may be living, or she might be dead." "Let us hope the former." "A hope that's full of dread," said Arnold Jackson.

CHAPTER VIII.

ART AND NATURE.—HARRY ANDERSON.

THE result of that chance meeting with Arnold Jackson was an intimate acquaintance, and a pecuniary advantage also, to Anderson; for as his pictures were really selling-looking ones, possessed of a certain degree of merit, and the work of his son's friend, the old man, finding he could get a good pull out of them, bought them readily; and even offered to pay him eighty pounds a year, for three years, to paint for him, with a certain share, in the third year, of the proceeds of such of his pictures as might be publicly exhibited and sold.

"Don't you be a fool," said Arnold, seeing that Harry was inclined to jump at it. "You stick on your own hook, old fellow. My father is right enough for his own side, but he is an awful cutter of corns, I can tell you. Eighty now is all very well as you stand in your shoes at the present time; but if you are worth that to him this year, what will you be next year, and how much more the third year—eh? Besides, yours would have to be pictures, not patchwork.

"Why, he has got a lot of poor beggars there, in the Waterloo Road, at a place of ours—clever fellows all of them, but tied to patching—each with his nose to the grindstone. He got hold of them at fifteen shillings, and a pound a week; and though they have been years with us, the best of them even now gets but his thirty shillings a week, although he is at it all day long, and sometimes by gaslight, and turns them out quickly too. It's awfully hard lines. Oh, my father does screw them, I can tell you; poor old Sky Jack, and Jem, and Frank the Rippler, and all the lot, in fact, and yet they are sharp ones.

"'Sky Jack'—that's Jack Parsons—he puts in our skies, and is no end of a sharp chap. He can move a brush if you like. It's a sweep, and a twist, and a mottle; and then, dust goes the softener, and in ten minutes pounds are on the picture! 'Purple Jem,' he's another—Jem Baker. He is our evening man, and puts in all the sunsets. It's wonderful how those purples fetch the public. 'Moo Dick,' he is clever too, Dick Harrison; uncommonly good at cattle —he and 'the Rustic'—that's little Tim Tappleton, work together; in fact, for the matter of that, they all do—It's this way, Harry.

"The old man, as you can see, is a

sharp one—he was born before daylight,
and has been up early since. Well, amongst
the pictures sent to our place for sale, our
rooms, not Bond Street—there are of course
lots of duffers, awful duffers; and the
greater the duffer the better the frame.
'Duff,' as we call him—he is one of our
men—sees to those things, he has his instruc-
tions; and unless some fellow is caught by
the frame, when Duff runs him up stiffish,
down goes the hammer to Duff. So that
very often, when the sale is over, there are
half-a-dozen or more brand-new frames—
good Alhambra ones very likely, ready for
the next sale, and Duff sees to them,
'the Waterloo lot,' as he calls them. The
result is this; if the pictures won't work up,
they are wiped out with the turps rag, and
fresh ones painted; but if they will, then
each has a cut at them.

"Say the subject is a green wood, bright

green and staring, with a cold blue sky
that is all about the picture. Slap Jem
goes with the purples through the branches,
and blurs the foliage; then dabs the sun,
the setting sun you know, low down and red;
then twists his sunset tints across the
canvass, with splash in foreground for a bit
of water. The Rustic sticks the gipsies
in or what not, and Ben, 'the finisher,' he
tones the lot.

"And if we want a river bit, or pair,
Frank Lee, 'the Rippler,' gets his innings
then : he's good at water. Jack's fine at
morning skies, and 'Grass' at meadows,—
Joe Reeves—he does the dewy business and
long shadows, and so is good for mornings
and for evenings—a useful fellow. I'll take
you there; I think you'll be amused. One
starts the picture, and it passes round; and
when Ben gets it, then it's out of hand:
view so-and-so, and 'painted on the spot'

—the 'spot,' or plot, on which our place is built."

"An explanation not found in the catalogues." "Just so," said Jackson. "Sometimes, however, it comes back again. If so, they alter it ; for if we offer the same frame and canvass, the picture's different each time we sell." "But about those Exhibition ones," said Anderson, "there would be a pull there, you know." "Not so much as you think," was the reply, "for the governor would take it out of you in the frames. We make them." "Well, one year then ?"

"The old man would not see it. It is in the three where he gets all the profit. Stick as you are, and sell them to him singly. The price will rise, you'll find, when you exhibit, and that you must do. Why, when they first hung me, my pictures fetched no more than yours—that is, at least, what father gets for yours. I went in for little five-guinea bits, simply to be known as an exhibitor; and now, although it is only eight years since I first showed— I was but twenty then—they have hung me at the Academy this year, as you know, and they did so last year, and in a fair place too, neither skied nor floored; and I can get my five-and-twenty or thirty guineas for a 24 × 18.

" Now look here, old fellow," said Jackson. " You can do nothing at present, not in town at least; they are all too close for you; so you had better go in for the provinces, and send to New Street for the Spring one. That would give you till about the middle of March for sending in. It is a good place, too, and a famous selling place. Will you say there, then, for your first walling — March next ? "

" If you like," said Anderson. So it was

settled, and a subject was soon after decided on.

Meantime, while the picture was progressing, Harry continued, for the sake of a little pocket-money by his own exertions, to sell to Jackson; and as he never pushed the old man for price, as his more needy brethren were obliged to do, he soon became a favourite, and ere long a frequent visitor at Dulwich—for he had pleasant manners and was a good listener—and a welcome dropper-in at Bond Street, where "Jemmy" was always to be found, within certain hours, extolling the charms of the picture he was selling, or depreciating the quality of those offered him, that he might knock the price down.

"No, sir, no," he would say, as he settled the sit of his velvet skull-cap and adjusted the gold-rimmed glasses to the curve of his eagle-nose; "No, sir, no; I could not touch it; I couldn't indeed. No, sir," holding the picture further in front of him, and elevating his chin to the desired angle, "the more I look at it, the more I can see there is a decided want of tone about it. It lacks breadth, too, and harmony. You can leave it if you like, sir; we have a first-class sale on next month, but I could not put a price upon it; money is tight just now, very tight indeed." And the picture would be left, and bought then at his own price, or cheapened and bought at once.

But if it was selling instead of buying, then the quiet, confidential, and decidedly satisfied manner he could assume was most amusing. "Without exception, sir," he would remark, "it is the finest specimen of the Master I ever possessed. I have had, I think I may say, sir, in my time, the cream of many collections—mine has been a large experience, sir—but such quality as you

have there is rare, very rare, at the price,
sir; but I bought it right, yes, I bought it
right. The gentleman from whom I obtained
it, though he had a fine collection and was
fairly versed in Art, had not that critical
knowledge of it that enables one to tell a
gem at a glance. However, if I can turn
my money with a fair profit—a fair profit,
sir—I am always contented. As I always
impress upon my son, sir, it is of no use
to be too grasping; you defeat your object.
Were not I, as you see, sir, piled up with
pictures, I should be tempted to keep it, if
only for the mere pleasure of always having
at hand a really good-class work to look
at."

But if the customer did not close at that,
more was added to it. "You know my
place? Dulwich, sir, Dulwich; Leigh Lodge,
Dulwich, within a stone's throw of the
Picture Gallery. Come and pick a bone

with me there, and we will have a look at
the Murillos, and you will see, sir, in those
master-pieces the same mellow tones that
here are so closely imitated.

"Here is another, sir, a landscape, a grand
landscape. There's a sky, sir; the luminous
look of it is wonderful! Bear it in your eye,
sir, and when we examine the Murillos we will
have a feast with the Cuyps, and you will
see how magical is the similarity. The ex-
traordinary way in which he has approached
the tone of the old Master is marvellous. It
is such a picture that, as I said by that one,
sir, money should not purchase it, were I
not full, quite full. If you decide on the
pair, sir, you cannot do wrong, I can assure
you; they are an acquisition to any gallery,
and will always hold money together."

The old man had another bait also for
loose cash; for when a customer failed to be
impressed with the importance of not losing

such a chance of acquiring good pictures, Jemmy would usher him into the long room at the back—his antique-furniture place—where the light was kept so nicely subdued, that flaws were not visible. "Now there is a little lot here, sir," he would remark, "that I should just like you to see—not to tempt you, sir, not to tempt you, but that you may see for yourself what genuine old stuff really is. I think you will say you don't see such every day. There, sir, look at these. Not much mistake as to their genuineness, I think. See, sir," he would say as he turned the chairs over with a rap on the floor, to shake the sawdust out. "There's the proof: worm-holed, you see, sir, worm-holed; none of your 'modern-antiques,' I am too old a hand to be caught by that stuff, and there is plenty of it made in town, I can assure you."

He was right; for the man at the little

shop on the left-hand side by Vauxhall Bridge was a dab hand at that sort of thing, and turned it out well, and to any age, drilled-holes included—and he worked for Jackson.

Yes, his son was right when he said the old man got up early. . He knew "his way about town" well, remarkably well, did Jemmy Jackson; there was no mistake on that point. As he used to say to his son, "the early bird gets the worm, and the man who has all his teeth in his head has the best bite." But Arnold, who had long been emancipated from the tricks and turns of trade, paid little heed to it, for his pictures brought him in a little independency. That his father was a great screw was certain ; and it was constantly being made manifest in more ways than one.

"What's that model cost you now, my lad ?" said he one day to Arnold, alluding to a fine-grown girl who figured in most of his pictures. "A pound a week, father, and cheap at the money. Her face sells the pictures." "Ah!" groaned he, at what he thought was the dire extravagance of the remuneration, "over fifty pounds a year. You'll never get rich at that rate. It's too much, quite too much. Now, I'll tell you what I'll do, Arnold. I have been thinking, as I can get one at half the money, that if you and I can stable our horses together, we may both save money by it—you let me have a picture out of them now and then as my share, and I'll find the model—find you one for nothing— there now !"

"You will, father?" "Yes! and with quite as selling-looking a face as the one you have now. Miss Hemming, who is with your mother, my boy, is going to leave; and I have seen a young girl—a very nice girl too, she is, who is willing to supply her place, as she will be shortly leaving her situation. She is a good reader and a good nurse; handy with her needle, quite respectable, and very domesticated"—Mrs. Jackson was a permanent invalid—"and as she has a fine face, and a good figure, and is tall and well made, she will be just the thing for you; and her's will be a fresh face for your customers."

"But I could not," said Arnold, "ask her to sit for me, father." "Oh, nonsense," said the old man. "She will feel flattered at first by your requesting her to do so, as you can say, and say truly, it will be for an exhibition picture; and then, as it is sure to be admired, we can easily make it a regular thing afterwards, when your mother is sleeping, or she can spare her. It will save your pocket and perhaps help mine."

So as Arnold knew Best, his chum, would be glad of the chance of his present model at the same terms as he paid her, the

arrangement was concluded ; but though
Jemmy thereby cleared a very considerable
surplus on the salary of the new "companion," the time came when he bitterly
repented ever putting on the screw in that
direction ; for when, in a few years afterwards, he wanted his son to try to win
the affections of the rich Miss Chamberlain
—a snub-nosed girl he hated—and so get
settled, he had to know that he was "settled"
already ; for constant association with the
pretty companion, as the pretty "model,"
had changed her name to Mrs. Arnold
Jackson.

So Arnold's home from then knew him
no more. It was just when Harry first
knew Arnold that she came to Dulwich,
and four years afterwards she changed
her name.

The picture that Harry Anderson painted
for the Spring Exhibition—" A lane scene

in Surrey"—and which was really Croxted Lane, Lower Dulwich, beloved of " couples," and known to Arnold and the pretty model, obtained in the Birmingham Exhibition a good place on the walls, in the large circular room, and sold, for there was good work in it ; and what with selling to Jackson and selling at the different galleries in the season, with little commissions as time went on, he soon made progress, for his own name to a picture became worth money.

At his father's death, three years before the date of our story, and which event left Harry in a comfortable position, for his father had saved money, he left the old studio in Fitzroy Square for one more cosy, though at a lower rental, in St. John's Wood. There he remained until the house had to come down for the railway ; when, meeting with a fine floor with a good light, in North Audley Street, and a nice little box at

Notting Hill, near Holland Park, he took the former for his studio, and the latter for his residence; and there it was that he lived at the time we know him.

A very pretty place—so said his uncle.

CHAPTER IX.

THE MEETING IN THE WOOD.—A WELCOME
SHOWER.

HARRY'S uncle, the Rev. Charles Arundell, for the past four years Rector of
Eymor, was a fine gentlemanly man, and
fifty years of age ; who, from the good he
did in his parish, and the quiet and unos-
tentatious way in which he did it, had
secured the goodwill and the good words of
all around him.

From his dignified demeanour and his
upright carriage as he went about his parish,
those who were strangers to him might

imagine him to be proud and haughty, and
one too who could scarcely condescend to
say more to his poorer parishioners than he
was obliged to do ; one from whom they
would doubtless obtain a sufficiency of tracts
and sermonising in the shape of advice and
homilies, but little else ; no sympathy with
their little troubles, no interest in their
daily doings ; one to whom they would
listen on a Sunday more from a dim sense
of duty, and a wholesome fear of a visit
from " the parson," than from the slightest
hope of any real comfort or consolation they
might gain by it.

But though such an estimate of character
might be very true of the rector in the
adjoining parish—Upperton, it was not so
of Mr. Arundell, for he was as tolerant and
sociable as the Rev. Martin Murray was
imperious and bigoted ; so while Eymor
Church was filled, Upperton was empty, for

people in country parishes will blend their religion with their likings ; and no matter how orthodox a man may be in the pulpit, if he wishes to secure a country congregation he must first be popular. Mr. Arundell was popular, and deservedly so.

You might see that on any Sunday morning, for as the sweet cadence of the bells, chiming for church, "just one, two, three, four, five ; just one, two, three, four, five," sent its melody to the hills, the cottagers would be seen making their way down the common through the ferns and the gorse, and trending churchwards, along the paths through the village ; for Eymor church, unlike so many others, was well filled, "wet or dry," as all who could go, did go, and they liked to go. The simple earnestness of the service was its charm, the "fatherly" utterance of the preacher was its welcome. What they heard they could

understand, for the sermons were plain and
homely and suited to their capacity. There
were no learned disquisitions to puzzle them,
no hard words to bother them. As they
themselves said, it was more like talking
quietly and kindly to them, as he did in
their cottages, than "regular sermons;" and
the way in which he explained things, "in
a rasonable sort o' a manner," made them
feel "a' the better, an' more comfortable
loike, fur thun hearin' on it."

Not that the worthy rector was incapable
of higher efforts, far from it, for in the
literary world, the name of Charles Arundell
was a name well known; but knowing his
congregation, he had the good sense also to
know that homely words best suited homely
people; and therefore it was, that he preached
not up to the level of his educated hearers,
but down to the level of his poorer ones, and
he was liked accordingly.

He was liked too for his genial manner and his homely ways, that made him bend down and chat to the little toddlers in the lanes, and that induced him to linger amongst the haycocks or between the sheaves, to gossip with the workers, and to loiter by the cribs to talk to the pickers. And the way in which he would potter about amongst those wonderful tangled-up gardens on the common, and in the village, where flowers and bushes struggled for the mastery, and listen time after time to the separate history of every plant, and how this was coming into blossom, and that was budding, delighted the old women beyond measure, who confided to him all their woes and all their ailments, and invariably obtained from him commiseration for the one, and due sympathy for the other ; their harrowing details as to the failing state of their extremities, rheumatics and the colic, never seeming to weary him.

To ask in a country parish about somebody's "poor leg" is a great point, though
not a safe one, for the clergyman is shown
it on the instant as readily as the doctor;
and to remember the divers ailments there
of divers people brings certain commenda-
tion to the memory man, and indeed goes
further in their estimation than book-learn-
ing, long words, proper names, or Meso-
potamia. To Mr. Arundell thought and
inquiry, however, came naturally — good
offices and good words developed themselves
spontaneously.

Anne, his wife, some years younger than
himself, was an invalid, and had been so
for many years; for the death of her sister,
Mrs. George Anderson, told on her, so that
her visitings amongst the poor had to be
few and far between; but "the miss of
her," as the old people said, would have
been greater had not it been for the atten-

tion and kindness they all received from her daughter Clara, who at the time at which our narrative commences was nineteen, one year younger than Nelly, whose bosom friend she was, for they were kindred spirits—in all good works at least—and from Emma, who was seventeen; tall girls each of them, and favoured with good looks. Clara was a fair-haired girl, and Emma had dark hair, the same as her brother "Willie," the only son, who, not liking the Church, had been placed with an architect in London, and was now twenty-one.

The Rectory was a good substantial house, and large and roomy, well furnished inside and picturesque outside, with lawn, dressed ground, and shrubberies, sloping up from the Church lane; with a good-sized meadow by it, and a paddock and some orchards at the back of it.

Soon after his father's death — twelve

months after Mr. Arundell came to Eymor
—Harry Anderson paid his first visit to the
Rectory, and he was then well pleased with
the place and the neighbourhood. He was
there for a week or two, as his father had
left to Mr. Arundell the bulk of his pictures
—good works by good masters—and Harry
was asked to assist in the hanging of them
and in the necessary re-arrangement of those
his uncle already possessed.

The following summer he was again there,
sketching in the woods; but on neither
occasion did Nelly meet with him, for she
was in London with her aunts Hamilton the
first time, and at Brighton with her uncle,
Dr. James Hamilton, the next time; so that
it was not until Anderson's third visit,
eighteen months ago, that Nelly became
acquainted with him; and it was then in
May, that charming month of sweet associa-
tions—the hawthorn-scented apple month of

May—that he again came to the Rectory, to have a sniff of the hawthorns, a sight of the apple bloom, some trout-fishing in the river, and some sketching in the woods; and perhaps some evening rambles with his pretty cousins for glow-worms and nightingales.

What a month May is, with its deeper greens and many brighter colours! How gladly do we welcome its fine days and sunny skies, now that the showers of April are no longer treacherous, and we can prolong our walks without a wetting.

And what walks those are when in a woodland country; for you have then merely to stroll through the woods or the copses, to understand what "carpeted with flowers" really means; you have only to wander through the meadows, to know that "ankle-deep in blossoms" is a fact, not a fancy; and if you take a turn about the commons,

"golden gorse" will be present to you on a
hundred bushes; and as for "sheets of
colour," go into the hamlets of Herefordshire, or better still, into that long stretching
valley which separates them from the elm-
treed lanes of Worcestershire—"The Golden
Valley," the valley of the Teme; and in the
miles and miles of orcharding that you
will see there, in this glorious month of
May, you will recognise the truth of it.
Talk of "rose and snow!" well there it is,
in all its dainty tenderness of tint.

It is only in an orchard country that we
can fully realise the extreme beauty of the
apple-blossom; it is only there that we can
get such wafts of the scent of it. Fancy,
wandering through orchard after orchard
under the apple trees, when all their grey
boughs meet in heaps above you, and each
mossed trunk is topped with clumps of blossom
—now rose, now white, then red-and-white,

or red; with the soft bloom coming flush against the blue, as you look up through the twisted twigs to the bright sky over; while falling petals, fluttering by your face, chequer the deep greens of the lush grass under.

Fancy hawthorn hedges too, to those miles of orchards—say the middle of May, for then they are thick with pearly buds and blossoms. Hawthorn and apple bloom! That if you like is a smell worth smelling.

But to get a really good sniff of hawthorn only, you should go out on a May evening, just as the moon is rising, and have a turn or two through cowslip meadows, and high-hedged old lanes, to listen to the nightingales, and search for lady glow-worms in the grass, whose green lights guide you. You will then get sweet scent and music too; and such music and such scent, that you will like to linger.

But if you don't turn out at night, be
"up in the morning early," while the dew
is on the bushes, and try that. You will
need no guide then to tell you where the
hawthorns are. And if you are a fisherman,
take your rod with you, and go down to
the quiet spots by the fishing-fords, and you
will see the trout there darting at the May
fly, or poising, motionless, over their shadows
on the sand. And should you come back
with a few of them, and have them for
your breakfast, you will know what a relish
is. Trout, cooked as soon as caught, are
not bad things.

That, by the way, though, for your real
pleasure in thus turning out so early, will
be the walk you will have there, and the
sights you will see; for an early walk in
the country on a bright May morning is
one of the enjoyable things of this world;
especially if you start at daybreak, and

before the rooks, just as the yellow ripples through the grey, to watch the views unfold, as gold and amber scatters into blue, for then the fresh smell of the hawthorn hedges that comes to you is most delicious; and the cry of the cuckoo, and the twittering of the birds, as they are waking up in the bushes, are the only sounds you hear.

Sketching in the woods too, how jolly that is in May; when you have left the hot and dusty crowded streets in town, for the tranquil beauty of the country—for its welcome solitude, so calm, so quiet! What a delightful sense of freedom one gets when first we watch the sunlight through the leaves, and see the shimmering greys on great green trees, the soft blue mistiness in woods and hollows; the vast expanse of sky, the flood of light, the moving clouds, and ever-creeping shadows!

How each step we take in our journey

onwards makes us wish more and more for
the company of our friends in town, if only
just to see what they would think of it,
and to share their wonderment, as we look
across the valley to the grand old hills!
How dim the light is where the woods are
thick! what golden gleams lie flickering
on the path, where thinner leafage lets the
sunshine through, and makes white lights
on ferns, and shaking shadows on the grey
tree-trunks!

With what satisfaction, having taken our
stand-point, do we fix our easel, and then
set to work; listening the while to the caw
of the rooks and the cooing of the doves,
as we move our brush mechanically, to the
" chip cheep, twit tweet," of the bird on the
bough, that rings out as we touch in the
foliage; or the " peep, peep, pip," that keeps
time as we mark in the branches, and comes
clear, like a key on an anvil! How earnestly

and with what a loving hand do we try to depict that which is before us ; and how constantly do we catch ourselves yielding to the charm of stopping to gaze at some fresh effects, some new and sudden beauties, instead of trying then and there to fix their fleeting forms upon the canvass !

How that link of love between ourselves and Nature makes us recognise the beautiful; how it makes our senses gratified with common objects and with simplest scenes! What rest to wearied minds is in great woods; what joy in blue sky, white clouds, and high hills ; and what a calm in twilight distances and far-off country ; what peace in moonlit valleys with bright stars above them! The whole of Nature has a sunny side, and in all things there is some sort of beauty— a quiet pleasure too in observation.

And this love of Nature, and this charm of observation, which is so inherent with all artists, was markedly so with Anderson, who never could get away into the woods without realising it in all its intensity; and it was on one of those warm May days of bright and balmy weather—enticing one to woods, green lanes, and fields—that, coming to the Rectory overnight, after a stay in town for the first week at the Academy, he was induced to turn out early with easel and umbrella, and make a pitch in the Home Wood, for the sake of a long green glade he saw when last he was there.

Just as he had made his sketch, and was getting in his chequered lights and shadows, a rustle ahead of him, and the sound of a musical voice, made him look up, brush in hand, in the direction of it. A black pony trotted up the bank, neighed, and stopped; and after him, with hat in hand, and all her curls a-blowing, a girl with riding-whip and simply dressed—grey habit and black hat, red rose, white collar—who came laughing and scrambling through the ferns and the bushes to cut off his retreat with, "Oh, you naughty pony! that is the way you serve me, is it, for easing you up the bank? I shall have something to say to you when I do catch you."

"Oh, pray don't scold him, he's a pretty pony," said Harry, as he caught him, as she came. Blushing at so unexpected a meeting with a gentleman, she thanked him, and at once asked if she might look at the picture he was painting. "Yes," said she, critically scrutinising it, "it comes famously. I sketched that once myself, but from this point it comes better. I tell papa it is the prettiest bit in the wood." "Miss Hamilton, I think?" said Harry, raising his hat to her. "Yes—Nelly." "I see; the little lady who is such a sketcher. My uncle spoke of you—my uncle at the Rectory—

my name is Anderson. I fear I am tres-
passing. I should have asked permission
of your father." "Oh, not at all! He will
be very pleased about it. He always is
when people come to sketch. But pray don't
let me hinder you, Mr. Anderson," said
Nelly, taking the pony by the bridle; "if
you will allow me, I will just stay a few
minutes, while this naughty pony gets
his breath, and watch you paint."

So then there was a gossip between them,
to their mutual satisfaction; when Nelly,
hearing the patter of rain-drops on the
leaves over them, said she must be going;
but Anderson, assuring her that it would
soon be over, turned his canvass, and moved,
with her and the pony, to the shelter of
an old yew, whose great black branches
stretched there down below them, and whose
hollowed trunk could shelter many people.
Slipping the reins round the crutch of the

saddle, Nelly told White-face to behave himself, and pushing him into the trunk of the tree, she and Harry sat down on the roots of it—great gnarled ones running all about the bank.

For an hour or more, however, it rained fast, but time passed quickly. "Hark! there's the cuckoo. I'll turn my money," Harry said; "'tis lucky when first you hear him." "They say," said Nelly, "too, that what you are doing then you will do all the year." "Ah! do they? Well, I am very glad of that." "You are fond of painting then?" "Yes, and shall be fonder when I, as then, have with it thoughts of you, which now I must have 'all the year,' you know." "Of me!" said Nelly. "Yes, you, Miss Hamilton; I was thinking earnestly of you just when I heard him—nay, you looked so charming that I could not help it." "Oh! Mr. Anderson, how you

do flatter!" "No flattery. That wretched
bird is now a blessed bird; I'll call him
names no more." "But don't you like to
hear the cuckoo's cry?" "I never have
done so; he used, in fact, to madden me
and stop my brush; and I have often wished
to do as the Italians do—catch him, and
roast him, and eat him. But now, as his
cry, Miss Hamilton, will but recall a
pleasant meeting, and—may I hope?—a
still pleasanter acquaintance, I shall ever
welcome him, and do violence to my
feelings for the sake of the association, by
trying to fancy his monotonous cry quite
musical."

"Oh, don't do that. I am but a country
girl; that's why I like him." "And also
why at first sight I like you. I knew I
should, from what my cousins said. You
country girls are all so natural: after a spell
in town 'tis quite refreshing. Now look at

Clara; is she not a love? Impulse and innocence, and all that's artless. And Emma also." "She is, indeed; and so is Emma too. I do love Clara, but I am fond of both." "I wish you could but make it three in time, and link me with them." "I think I must be going," Nelly said. "Oh, don't go yet; the rain is not half over." "Oh yes, it is." "Not quite, I think; I thought I felt a spot. At all events, the storm may come again. I think you had better wait a little longer." "Oh, no, I am sure 'tis over. Papa will think me very long away. I only hinder you." "A sort of hindrance I should like each day. Allow me, please." "Thanks," Nell said, as she mounted.

"I will see you through the wood, if you'll permit me; the gates are awkward." "Oh, pray don't trouble. I am used to them; I am through them daily, to see the people up there on the common." "You will be, then, through to-morrow?" "Yes, I shall, but not this way, at least I think not." "Well, if you should, Miss Hamilton, I should be very pleased indeed to show you—as you seem to like pictures—what progress I have made with mine by then. I daresay the girls will be with me; Clara if not Emma." "Thanks; will they? Well, I'll see. I do like pictures, so—perhaps I may." "I hope you will," said Harry Anderson.

"She is very plain, and yet I like her looks," thought he, while watching her till out of sight. "A winsome little lady, frank and natural, with heart untouched, and with sweet winning ways. I have half a mind to paint her and the pony. By Jove, I will! A reminiscence, just a memory." With that he set to work, and soon had

White-face, blowing curls and all; a sketchy bit, but like both Nell and him.

"A pleasant, gentlemanly man, and clever," was Nelly's verdict as she cantered home.

CHAPTER X.

THE RECTOR'S OFFER.—"AH, LOOK AT THAT!" SAID JOE.

THE next morning she rode by the Rectory, and called there to ask Miss Arundell if she would come for a ride; professedly so at least, but really—discreet and timorous— to avoid another chance meeting with Harry only, by learning if Clara or Emma had gone with him. "Yes," said Clara, who was busy with her flowers, "and we will go up to the wood if you like. Harry is there painting." So they went; and the picture was shown to them, and the sketch too, which soon set Nelly blushing. "Oh, you sly puss!" said Clara; "you never told me." "You did not ask me," said Nelly. "Never tell tales out of school, Miss Hamilton," said Harry, laughing. "I like to cherish pleasant recollections. Can you forgive me?" "She ought to do so," said Clara, interposing, "for it shows she made an impression on you." "The pony, not I. Yes, you, you beauty," said Nelly, colouring, as she patted White-face. "Both," said Harry, "but one in particular." So Clara laughed, and made Nell's colour deeper.

After a pleasant chat, and much artistic gossip, they left Harry to his own devices, and trotted on. But in the evening, having promised Clara to come down there to tea, Nelly again found herself alongside the painter; and Mr. Arundell—Art being with him a kindred topic also—seated himself beside them, and, joining in the conversa-

tion, soon elicited from Nelly her love of
the beautiful and her own knowledge of
Art belongings; while Harry, charmed with
her enthusiasm and artless manner, watched
her bright face, and thought how very
pleasing some plain features are when lit
up with unstudied animation. "You must
come and see my pictures, Miss Nelly," said
the Rector, rising. "I think there are a
few fresh ones since last you saw them;
and I got hold of a bit of tapestry the
other day—thanks to Harry here—and some
china."

So they went up-stairs into the long-room,
three rooms thrown into one, and Harry
was the showman. It was not a large lot,
certainly, but those he had were good. A
Wilkie and Wouvermans, Watteau and Win-
terhalter; Reubens and Reynolds; a Sant and
Schlesinger; Lancret and Lawrence, Van
Huysum and Vernet; a Millais and Metzu,

Jardin and Gerome; Berghem and Bonheur, Frith and Fragonard; a Claude and Cooper, Nasmyth and O'Neil; Mieris and a Meisonnier, a sketch—a gem; and sundry others also, well worth looking at; including an Arthur Gilbert, some small David Cox's, and a charming water-colour by Birket Foster.

And in a room opening out of the long-room, was what he called his "Vernon Gallery," all oils, and consisting of some fine Welsh views and autumn scenes by the father, W. H. Vernon—a friend of Mr. Arundell, and a man of note; and a series of clever pictures by his daughters, "the Vernon family," of whom Nelly had often heard in Art circles, and whose fame, indeed, and the way in which they had used their talent to advantage, first fired her with the laudable desire to go and do likewise. But she had yet to learn "oil," for she was only a water-colourist.

After they had looked at the pictures, and inspected the tapestry—a 17th century bit of old Spanish, and an upright panel of Gobelins, duly signed, the old cabinets, and the Majolica ware and the china, they returned down-stairs; when the Rector and Harry, with the ladies alongside them, and with Mrs. Arundell looking on from the sofa, proceeded to inspect some of Nelly's drawings, which—her friend Clara, being seized, as she said, with a sudden desire to paint—she had brought with her, as requested, that they might serve " for copies." Such at least was the reason given to Nelly by Harry's clever cousin.

" Aye," said Harry, as he looked at them, " these are something like; I like these. Pure untouched studies; rough, vigorous, and true; no mere feminine prettinesses; the shadows glazed, the colours touched to stand, each in its place, unmuddled and unmixed." "They are just as I did them," said Nelly; "mere views near home. I always use that granulated paper; I like it best." "Yes, you are right, Miss Hamilton; it gives texture, and helps your atmosphere, and makes your picture suggestive; so full of indications for those accidentals that come with touches, as your own eyes see them."

"And how you can see them!" said Nelly warmly. "Why when I look into some of even those rough things, I declare I could finish them up quite highly, forms come so clearly. Mere splashes, ferns; a lot of spottlings, rooks; a blot, a figure; and a miss, some sheep. Is it not nice, too, when you are in the woods, to look with half-closed eyes at bits of beauty, and so enhance them by thus blending form? It gives such breadth."

"It is," said Harry, "and what I often do; with gradual closure, all the lights tone

down, bright sun to twilight. You find out
by it too, if you are painting, the effect that
best will suit each sketch you make. Besides,
'tis jolly—of one view you make three, or
four, or five, each light a difference, just
while you see it. I often lie and look down
through the trees, and fade the light till
forms blend into mist. But you should
try oil, Miss Hamilton; yours is a good
broad touch, with no niggling nonsense
about it, and you would soon manage it. I
am sure you would like it." "I don't know
that," replied Nelly; "it seems such dirty
work. But if I thought I ever should
succeed in it, I would try it, however;
that is, if papa would set me up with the
requisites."

"Oh, I have an easel and colours," said
the Rector, "and I think some odd canvasses,
if I can just lay my hands on them; so if

you would like to try your hand Miss Nelly, now is your time. They are at your service, and Harry here could have a look to you while he is staying with us." "I should have great pleasure, uncle, I am sure, in doing so ; and anything of which I could inform Miss Hamilton, I should be glad to tell her." "I am much obliged to you, Mr. Anderson, you are very kind, but I fear you would find me but a stupid pupil ; and I could not think, Mr. Arundell, of using your colours in that way." "Well, for the matter of that, Miss Nelly, I think the best thing I can do will be to transfer to you the lot, bodily—box, easel, and oddments— for I don't suppose I shall ever paint again, and my girls here have no taste for it ; they are merely paper-stainers." "Papa ! how can you ?" cried both the girls at once. "Oh, Clara," said Nelly, "is going to learn landscapes, I brought these for her ; she said—now did you not ?—that she would copy them."

"When Harry goes, her impulse will be gone, at least I think so ; but if you get on yourself," said the Rector, "and learn oil, you can then teach her ; so you will please, Miss Nelly, let me send my traps up, for you to do as you like with them ; and if I can find a few old canvasses, they will do for you to commence with. We shall be up to-morrow, should nothing prevent us. I must introduce Harry to your father, for though he has paid us a visit or two, they have not yet met ; and we will then have a chat about things, and put you into the way of it. Harry, of course, knows far more about that sort of thing than I do, and whenever he can come and see us, I know he will be pleased to have a look to you, and tell you anything you want to know."   " Delighted, uncle, I am sure, at any time, if I can be of the least service to Miss Hamilton."

And thus it came about that Nelly's progress in Art was advanced a stage, and a pretext furnished her for the future—if such were wanted—for those pleasant gossiping times, and that closer intimacy with Anderson, which was the outcome of that meeting in the wood. From kindred tastes come kindred sympathies—and often sympathy awakens love.

Harry on the morrow went up to Eymor House, and he was warmly welcomed by the Hamiltons, to whom he was introduced by the Rector ; and a croquet party was at once organised for the evening, as Nelly's cousins, Fred and Annie, were coming from Bickley, with their father, " uncle Charles "—Charles Hamilton, a farmer, John's elder brother—to stay the night. The Rector was going out, but he promised for the ladies, who came with Harry.

And a very pleasant party it was, too, for Frank hunted up the umbrella tents, and gave them their first sunning; the gardener found sufficient strawberries in the hot-houses to make a visit to the dairy necessary; and claret-cup, concocted by knowing hands, was forthcoming at the proper time; and last, and not least, a dance by moonlight on the lawn was indulged in after supper, and prolonged late enough for them to hear the nightingales in the woods below in full song.

So sociable and so friendly were all there, that when Harry left that night, he seemed to have known them for years. "Frank," he said, "was a thoroughly good fellow; and, as for that uncle Charles," who was a widower, "he was the jolliest old boy he had met for many a day." Yes, he liked the

Hamiltons, certainly, on first acquaintance—
Nelly especially.

When he took Mrs. Hamilton down to
supper, and recognised Nelly's handiwork in
the floral decorations of the table, he had
an opportunity of saying that which he had
to say about her drawings ; and also, in the
course of the evening, of complimenting Miss
Aymes on the proficiency of her pupil. He
then elicited from her that she herself had
painted in oil ; and that she had, indeed,
some years ago, exhibited as an amateur for
several seasons ; and that the pictures thus
exhibited by her had been also sold.

Here, then, was an unexpected ally, could
her interest be gained, in the matter of Miss
Nelly's advancement in Art, and in further-
ance of his own wishes to be of service to
her ; for be it remembered Miss Aymes, as
governess, was still in authority, and it
would rest a good deal therefore with her

whether or not school hours could be sufficiently infringed upon during his visits to
the Rectory—and the thought crossed his
mind that he might be there oftener—to
allow of those little conferences with Miss
Hamilton which, under the plea of " instruction," seemed to him then as likely to
be very feasible and very pleasant.

When two people meet who have a love
of Art, they generally get on together very
well ; and with Miss Aymes, the time spent
in his company passed, with such a genial
topic for conversation, most pleasantly ; and
the impression he made upon her was a
favourable one—so favourable indeed, that if
Mr. and Mrs. Hamilton were agreeable, she
would, she said, at once see what· could be
done for her pupil, in that matter of easel
and canvasses.

The upshot of it was, that as the croquet
party had prevented the overhauling of the

odds and ends sent from the Rectory, Mr.
Hamilton asked Harry—as he would only be
painting in the morning, when he alone got
the effect of light he wanted—if he would
come down from the wood on the morrow,
and have a bit of dinner with them, just in
a plain way; and he and Nelly could then
put their heads together, and see what they
could make of it; John Hamilton, looking
on it in a "master and pupil" light only,
as he, Anderson, was at that time eight-and-
twenty, while Nelly was but eighteen. Was
he quite sure it would not be hindering
him? Yes, quite sure; in fact, if Miss
Hamilton would then like to commence some
little picture, he could at once see, from the
way she handled and moved her brush,
whether or not she would soon get into it.

The next morning, after the Bickley people
had left, Mr. Hamilton, who had been up
to the keeper's to see Mary about the mar-

keting, came back along the top of the
wood, and there stayed some time with
Anderson, watching him at work and gossiping, and they then went down to the house
together.   After dinner, the painting traps
were had out, a canvass of suitable size
selected, the easel was fixed, and the palette
set; and Nelly, with Harry by her, stood,
charcoal in hand, ready to sketch in the
salient points of the shed before her.

By the time she had laid in her sky and
got the shadows, her father and Miss Aymes
came to them; and in reply to their
respective inquiries, Anderson said that he
could see, with a little instruction from Miss
Aymes, Miss Hamilton would very soon
paint a picture. The handling was right
enough; it was simply a question of mate-
rial—oil instead of water; practice and
perseverance would do much. Then Nell
and Harry were left alone, as her father

thought they would get on better together
if they had no one by to bother them.
Miss Aymes went off to her ferns, and he
went round to the stables, as Frank was
away at a fair.

The old shed which was thus the subject
of her first canvass was, after sundry pleasant
"lessons," finished during Harry's stay at
the Rectory; and such a really creditable
picture did she make of it that, after a
good deal of pressure on his part, and an
assurance that if she would like to dispose
of it, he had no doubt he could find a
purchaser, the picture was consigned to his
care, and he took it back to town with
him.

As Mr. Hamilton entered the stable, old
Joe was forking the bed over, and as usual,
talking to himself; the purport of his soli-
loquy evidently being the painting of the
shed, and the belongings of the new visitor;

for with his accustomed perseverance and
tenacity of purpose, that was the subject
broached, and held to, when his master sat
down on the corn-bin and talked to him—
Joe being at all times a privileged individual, as, on account of his long services,
his little peculiarities were humoured, and
his remarks ignored.

"A wish ad a knowd," said he, "as the
young Missis wan agwain to tak that oud
shed, sur; a could a cut the ivvy clouse,
an a maide him toidy fur hur. Ud a
shoved a bit o' clane straw under it too,
to kivvir thun oud thatch on him; a be
got sa dirty; an a scraaped the moss off
him as ba lump-ed theer." "You would
have done mischief then, Joe," said Mr.
Hamilton, "as that is just the reason she
likes to sketch it." "Now bin it, sur? Sure!
Well a shoodna ha' thought it. But mebbe
sheen dress him hup i' the payntin on him,

an spruce him?" "Not a bit of it, Joe;
she will try to copy it exactly." "Sure,
sur! Look at that neow. Well that be
curus. An who be he sur as ba ooth hur?"
said Joe. "A sid 'm anow jist, as a went
inter the rick-yaard. A bin a angin aboot
these here paarts afore to-daay; but a
manes no harm a taake it, fur a inna sa
bad a lookin un." "Harm? Well, I should
say not, Joe. He is the parson's nephew."

"Ah, look at that neow! But a baynt a
comin to prache to we though, sur, bin 'm?
ecos a thinks his nut be saft, meyster; a
dunna think as a be quoite roight in his
yud." "Right, Joe? yes, as right as you are,"
said Mr. Hamilton. "Well," said Joe, " I
defers to you, sur, in coorse as be ma dooty,
but a ha' sid 'm a powerful lot o' toimes,
on an off, sur, a axshally a sitted down o'
the commin, an up i' thun ood, a taakin off
bits o' feern an things, an a puttin it o' paaper,

in a book. Now whaat could they ha' bin to
he, a oonder? An oonst a sid im i' the coppy
—no, it were i' thun ash-bed—a were agoin it
sollum loike at some burdock laves, an a
payntin on 'em green and yaller, on a whoite
rag, wi' a gallows thing i' the front on him,
loike the young missis han gotten. A oodna
a done that sur, ooda, ef a wan roight; nothin
but laves?

"An thin agin, sur," continued Joe,
" whoile a stood a waatchin on im, a putt
his pictur in a box, a flat un, an a screwed
him in, a good un; an a scraaped his paynt
wi' a big knoife, off that theer piece o' ood
as ad got, as ef he wan agwain to ate it, loike
jam; but a didna, fur a plaastered it o' the
grass, an maide it all sorts o' colours, quoite
pratty loike." "He is an artist, Joe," said
Mr. Hamilton, " you have heard of artists?"
"A dunna kneow as a an, meyster. What
sort o' cattle be em? A nivver heerd o' they."

"They are persons," was the reply, "who paint pictures. The pictures on that sheet almanack that I gave you to hang in the saddle-room are done by artists." "Ah, look at that neow!" said Joe. "Whoy a thought as how the printer ud putt them in hisself, jist ta amuse we chaps o' winter noights loike. Well, sure! Then the next orlmanaxt as we han, sur, mebbe ool han the feerns in, an the burdocks?" "Perhaps it will, Joe," said Mr. Hamilton, humouring him. "Well a ool saay this fur him," said Joe, "a sartinly wan rasonable in his talk, ef a wan quare, fur a axed ma to hev a bit o' bacco, an gin it ma, as free as yer loike— the Lord bless 'm fur it; but a conna maake out aboot them bits o' things nohow, darn ma body ef a con. Whoy a sis hapes an hapes on 'em aboot the farm, a does, an a nivver stops, a dunna, not a minute, to taake 'em off; theym sich common things. Now

ef it ud bin the young missis's pony, or
Foirefloy, or Sarcybooy, or some o' the cows
or the ship, whoy ud a said summut to
him."

"But he can take those off, as you call
it, quite as well as the ferns and things,
and so well, that you would know their
pictures in a minute, each one of them."

"'Now cooda, sur, sure?" said Joe. "Look
at that neow! Well, that be clever. A
shoon loike to taake them off mysen, fur a
be moighty fond o' they. An cooda atookt
the young missis too, on the pony, sur, or
when hur be agwain a 'untin'?"

"Oh yes, Joe, anything; horses, hounds,
fox and all, and you too."

"Lor, sur! now cooda? Whaat! taake
ma an ma oud smock too! Well, a must
be a rum un, that's sure. Whaatn all the
plaates, an the fancy work in 'm?"

"The whole smock-frock, perfect, Joe,

pleats and all." "Ah! look at that neow!
Thin, depind upon it, meyster, a be a good
un; theer's summut in 'm, that's sure,"
said Joe.

In a week after Harry Anderson returned
to Town, Mr. Hamilton had a letter from
him, inclosing a five-pound note "for Miss
Hamilton," the price he had put upon the
picture, which "a friend" had purchased.
The letter was encouraging. She had only
to go on, to succeed; and he had no doubt,
should she prefer to dispose of the pictures
she painted, that—if she would allow him
to do so—he could market them for her.

Here, then, was the prospect of a little
mine of wealth opened up to Nelly. Would
it not be jolly! because she could then—
and by her own exertions too—do so much
more for the old people and the little
invalids. Oh, she would make them so comfortable! It would be nice. Yes, she would

work now, that she would. It—yes, it
might—perhaps, please him too, if she could
succeed; and really, he had been kind, yes,
very kind.

So Nelly, aided and seconded by Miss
Aymes, settled to it, with a will; and, as is
generally the case with most people under
like circumstances, succeeded; and, between
the time we name and the date of our story,
she had painted and sold—through Harry's
good offices—several small pictures of places
in the neighbourhood.

Little did Nelly think, however, when
painting that first picture of the shed, where
and under what circumstances she would
again meet with it. "From little causes,
great events arise."

CHAPTER XI.

THE FIND—THE PROOF. "THAT WHITE FACE WAS NO FANCY."

HAVING now disposed of certain introductory matters, the narration of which was necessary for the better understanding of the events we shall describe, we will return to Lawson of Landimoor, and proceed with our story.

For a week or more, the doctor saw him daily, and twice a day; but though, through skill and care, an increase of brain symptoms was prevented, he still continued in the same dazed state, muttering at intervals, and always brooding—that "white face" haunting him. "Time may better him," said the doctor, "but I don't think medicine will do much good—I have no great opinion of him either way. In fact, it is more than likely that he will continue in this childish state for some time; and if his mind in the end gives way altogether, we must not wonder at it. He has been a hard drinker, Hamilton, and softening of the brain may follow this mental shock. His fits of passion, extreme irritability, and his constant suspicion of those about him, together with his groundless antipathy to his daughter— to which, as I find, he has been a victim for some years—all point to mischief in the brain, which, though it may remain latent for a long time, when roused, as in his case, by some great shock, soon developes itself, and is not then easily combated.

"I will give him a look in from time to time, whenever I am in the neighbourhood, or you can send if he is worse; but as it is really, Hamilton, a case more for moral treatment, and good nursing, and proper management by those about him, than for anything I can do for him, it would be useless putting the poor fellow to unnecessary expense, or dosing him with physic. They must try to turn his thoughts, not name his daughter, the fire, or anything that would in any way bear on that night. Remorse is present, they must not increase it, or else I think you'll find it will end badly."

And thus it rested. The doctor saw him occasionally, all friends did their best, and Nelly was down there daily, with little niceties, or to ask about him; but though he did not get decidedly worse, he did not mend, but still continued in that same sad childish state. The few times he had been down-stairs, though he was worse for a while, each time, his glance going at once to the window, where he saw "the white face;" so Mr. Hamilton had it built up, and another opened on the opposite side, which made a casement on either side the door, and thus totally altered the appearance of the room; as instead of a cross light, there was then a bright light in front, and the rest was in shadow.

The first time or two after the alteration, he seemed puzzled, and went and felt against the new blank wall; then examined both the windows, inside and out; and first asked this question, and then asked that, to be each time put off with "dreaming, father; you have had an illness and are very weak—now sit you down a bit and don't you bother." They hoped in time to turn his thoughts so far, that he at last should think it but "a dream." The task was not so easy; it made him cunning,

and on the listen just to catch a word. He
felt they had tricked him, though he knew
not how.

Still that was better than his brooding
there from day to day, and often all day
long. Suspicion sharpened him; and though
at times remorse would seem to crush him,
its effects were counteracted by that feeling,
the constant wish to get the best of them,
to circumvent them. It also kept him often
on the move. He should like to know it
was only a dream, for the thoughts of it
frightened him so at night; but he wanted
to be "sure" about it. He was not going
to let them trick him, and that he would
let them see, for he would watch them, and
be as sharp as they were, every inch of it.
They were not going to get over old George
Lawson in a hurry.

Thus would his thoughts run, and at
times he would try to think it out for himself,

and to go back to old times, when his daughter was at home; but he never could make anything of it, it was all a jumble; nothing distinct, nothing tangible; so he watched and waited, sharpened up or trembled, just as it took him, or the fit was on him.

The matter, of course, got talked about, and it caused a good deal of gossip in the village; but as no one supposed for a moment that there was the least cause for Lawson's "fancy," his fright was set down as "a judgment" on him, for his previous goings on about his daughter, and his "tantrums" that night, when he was in drink. And in this opinion his own wife and young George most decidedly shared.

It was now February. A month had passed since that cold winter night; yet the snow that had been lying all that time, lay still; and all around there was as white

a world as when poor Jessie's home was
"home" no more. It was a severe winter,
one of the old-fashioned ones, and a stopper
for everything but a bit of skating and
some shooting; and now, so far as the
partridges and the pheasants were concerned,
that was over. No hunting, and no exer-
cising horses whatever, though the holly
was all down in the farm-houses; so they
had to remain in the stables and "eat their
heads off;" and a bit of carting and hedg-
ing work on the farm, or journeys to and
fro to the pits for coal for the poor, was
all that could be found for the men to do.

The only one at Eymor House who was
really satisfied with that state of things was
Nelly; but then she was always so easily
satisfied, and her daily journeyings on White-
face in the cold and bracing air, made her
feel brisk and sharp; and the continued
aspect of the country enabled her to paint

another snow scene, as a companion picture to the one she had finished. Had her old women and invalids been less cared for, it would have been very different, but they were warmly housed, fairly clad, and well seen to; and little Bessie, who seemed to be slowly sinking, was the only one about whom she was really anxious, as little Johnny Austen and Peter Bell's child were better.

It was a good time too for Bob, who was great at slides, and that keeping also of "the pot a-boiling," which by young enthusiasts is always felt to be so necessary when they get upon the ice; but, truth to tell, that weekly-boarder business was getting to be looked upon as rather a nuisance, it came too often; for until he was fairly off the ground again, there was no peace at Eymor; as, what with his teaching the magpie fresh words of town slang each week—which the wretched bird picked up readily, and never dropped again—and his getting off about the farm with young Tom, or off to Moss and the blacksmith, and his being also up to every possible mischief and feat of youthful daring, Bob was always being called to order or searched for, from the time he came home on the Saturday afternoon till he left again on the Monday morning.

His mother deplored it, but his father laughed. "You will see him one of these days, mother," said he—for the muscular theory always asserted itself, "go across country, a good one." But Mrs. Hamilton thought there was "more in life than hunting;" and that there ought to be some limit to that "hammering" of the lads at school, to which Master Bob was so much addicted. Laura, being of a more gentle disposition, said her lessons daily, as a good child should, and was duly obedient to her sister Nelly.

The only event out of the ordinary
routine that had occurred to Nelly during
the past few weeks, was her visit with
Frank, on the thirteenth, to the Hunt ball
in Worcester; which, as usual, was a very
gay affair, and most enjoyable.

Frank was on the committee of management, and a main man in the disposition of
the decorations of the room, which, with its
profusion of flowers and lace, and mirrors
and muslin, its wreaths and evergreens, and
hunting trophies, only needed the moving
intermixture of the white dresses and the
scarlet coats to the music of Godfrey's band
for it to make a pretty setting to a pretty
scene. Nelly was delighted, and none the
less so that, as quietly and becomingly
dressed, she entered the ball-room resting
on the arm of her brother—himself in
scarlet—she met with Anderson, who had
come from Oxford—he was still with the

Camerons—to join some friends of his who were there from Henwick; and his cousin, William Arundell, was with him.

The ball made amends for the disappointment at the Rectory, for she found a pleasant partner in Anderson, and he took her in to supper. "This room is very close, Miss Hamilton," said Harry, as their first dance after supper ended and the heat increased. "I think were we to take a turn or two amongst the flowers yonder, we should get some cool air there. May I offer you my arm?" "Thanks," said Nelly, rising; "I was just thinking the same thing myself. It really is warm here." And with her arm through his, they passed into the conservatory.

Mere friends as yet, no loving words had ever passed between them, but each was aware of the friendly feeling of the other, for there had been the silent conversation

of the eyes and a warm hand-pressure at
their every parting. She liked him because
he was kind and clever, and he saw that
she liked him, for she was too simple-minded
and too open-hearted to be otherwise than
natural ; and he liked her for her confiding,
child-like ways and country freshness. The
sympathy begot by kindred tastes is soon
revealed—a tone, the slightest pressure of
the hand, the least inflection of the voice,
a glance, each tells the tale so easily trans-
lated. The half-hour that they spent together
in the shade there, in the delicious coolness
of the conservatory, was an eventful one
to each of them, as it was an earnest of a
warmer friendship between them than had
hitherto existed.

"You will come down then when the
frost goes," said Frank, as he left with
Nelly, "and let me give you a mount
or two, for a spin across our country?"

"Thanks for the offer, Frank, I will," said Harry.

"George," said Frank to young Lawson of Landimoor, one day when the snow was going, " father and I are just off down the dingles, for a shot or two, before the brooks are out; they are rising fast. Charles flushed a wood-cock this morning as he came back from post, so we might drop on him; and there are some snipe about too, by the heads of those springs. If you are not busy, will you come along and help to beat for us?"

"Yes," said George, "I can if you like, sir; there's nothing much doing just now, and father's quiet."

So Mr. Hamilton, Frank, George and Charles turned out; the former with their guns, and the latter as beaters, taking the springers with them—three famous dogs, low-sized ones, that always kept within easy distance, and never gave tongue. "Do you mind going across to those turnips first?" said Frank, as they were starting, "those quice are there again. Confound 'em, I should like to settle a few of them." "Anywhere," said his father, "that we can get something to shoot at." So the men and the dogs being kept back, they stole up to the hedgerow; but just as they had got their guns through the brambles, to blaze at the ruck of them, the snap of a twig set the birds flying, so it was a case of long-shot. "Wood-pigeons to your notice, governor," said Frank, as he saw some tumble, and he scrambled over the hedge for the victims; "was it my gun or yours?" "Well, the kill to me decidedly, but you might have lodged a pellet," so Frank laughed, and came back to him with three of them. "Catch hold," said he to Charles, "and open the crop, will you, and empty it, or the turnip leaves will taste them."

"I say, George, what's the best way to cook a pigeon?" "I can't say as I know, sir." "Then I'll tell you. Cut through the back lengthways when you have plucked him, and turn it down on each side level with the breast; then gridiron him, and as soon as he is done through and through, which he will be soon, butter, and pepper, and salt him, and eat him hot. That's the way to do it; but don't keep him too long on the fire, or he will be hard and black, and not worth a button, George." "He ought to be good, sir, that way," said Lawson. "Yes, and so he is, too. Put them in your pocket, and try it when you get home again. It will be a relish for your father."

"Now then, governor, if you'll keep your eyes open, and come on, you or I may settle that cock, perhaps. We will take that reedy bit first, and then work across that patch of

brown fern—where the snow has blown off—
for the snipe in the dingles; and mind,
George, as we cross the fern, that you and
Charles don't tread on one, for they lie close,
and you won't then see the colour of them.
Now then—are we ready?"

"Seek 'em, Rover; go along Springer;
find 'em out Sprightly—good dogs!" said
Frank; and the little fellows went away,
and bustled about as busy as bees; and so
hunted every inch of ground that no game
could escape them. "Here he is then!"
said Mr. Hamilton; and as the dogs searched
about brisker than ever, "Mark, cock!"
cried the beaters, and bang went the gun,
and down the bird dropped—Springer bring-
ing him. "That's one to you, father."
"Hold hard, Frank," was his response,
"there's a whistle! Wait till he's straight."
And as he spoke a snipe got up, zigzagged
from the beaters, and crossed the line of

fire. Calculating the speed of him, Frank fired ahead of him, and brought him down. "Well done, Frank," said his father, "you did that neatly. Steady now, and we shall get another as we go on."

"That's it, Rover! good dog, good dog, find 'em out. Push 'em up, Sprightly. Seek 'em, Springer." And as they got near to some dead sedge in a corner, up got another —a little jack snipe—and both fired, but missed him. "Confound that little beggar," said Frank, "I thought I had put a pellet in him." However, further on they had better luck, for when they got to the springs, another snipe got up, and fell to Frank's gun; and a third afterwards to his father's. That seemed to be about the lot of them, for it was good-bye after that; as, though the dogs searched about as briskly as ever, it was over.

"While we are here," said Frank, as they

got down to the end of the dingles, "you may as well go on, Charles, and see if the river is rising much; for it strikes me we shall have a big flood before long, by the look of the brooks, and we must keep an eye to those ewes and lambs, in case of a sudden rise. We lost six last year you know, before we could get to them." "Very well, sir," said the groom; and Frank and his father, and young George Lawson, went on with the dogs, to take a bit of furze on their way back, on the chance of some rabbits, or whatever else might offer there.

"I am glad to see that big drift going at last, sir," said George, as they got into some enclosures near the road—the very spot where Jessie was that night—"it has stopped my trig there for a long time. If you'll wait, Mr. Frank, I'll make a road over for you, and I can then hold your gun." So he clambered up the hedge-bank, and got over;

but as much of the drift on the north side the fence still remained there, he had no sooner set his foot upon it than down he went, dislodging a lot of it.

"Hillo, young man," said Frank, as he stood on the bank and passed the gun over, "you have had a soft fall, I think." "I have," said Lawson, who was sat under the hedge with a heap of snow on his back. "Mind how you come, sir, for it's very loose." But the warning came too late. Frank followed suit. "Well," said he, as he got to the bottom, "if the governor has the same luck, there won't be much snow left on this side the fence, that's very certain."

"Here," said he, getting up, "give me the gun, father—just hold mine, George, will you?—and let me lend you a hand; its awkward dropping." The old man, however, had a better time of it than either of them, though he did bring the snow down. "I have got the better of you two, any way," said Mr. Hamilton. "Yes," said Frank, "but you have lost your handkerchief in the process. Here," said he, as he hooked it off a spray with George's stick, and pitched it to him, "and a nice mess you have made of it."

"It is not mine," was the reply, as he felt in his pockets, and looked at it. "If it is not your own it is George's. Here, George! catch," said he, as he rolled it up into a ball and threw it to him. "Nor mine, sir," said George, as he undid it, and then threw it down again. "No, I'll carry the gun a bit, sir; you keep the stick," said he, as Frank offered to take it; "it will help you over the fences, and I am a better climber than you, sir."

So Frank went on, flirting up the handkerchief again with his stick as he did so, and dropping it on to Lawson, who kicked it from him as it fell again. "Stop a bit though, Mr. Frank," said he, "there's a name on it. I didn't see that. We shall perhaps find an owner for it."

"Good God!" said he, as he looked at it, and dropped upon the bank.

"Why, George!—Lawson, my good fellow!" cried Frank, turning short round, and seeing him with his face buried in his hands. "What's the matter? Not the gun, I hope! You are not shot, are you?" "Yes, to the heart!" said Lawson. "Read, read! but don't you speak to me, Mr. Frank, don't speak to me. Oh, my God! my God!" said he, as he rocked in agony from side to side.

Upon the handkerchief was "Jessie Jane!"

All words were useless. "Oh no, no!" said the poor fellow to Mr. Hamilton, "it's no use, sir, it's no use! You mean it kind, I know, but it's too plain, too plain! I see it all now clear enough, that 'white face' was no fancy. 'Twas Jessie come back home. She heard him curse her and she rushed off here. Drowned! for a certainty—poor girl, poor girl!

"But for that Lewis she might now be living. He—he, Mr. Frank it was who made her leave—her home and us—yes, he, the scoundrel! But if he and I should meet—yes, if we should meet again in this world—then—then, my poor sister, he shall answer for it!"

CHAPTER XII.

A BAD DAY'S BUSINESS, AND A NIGHT ALARM.

OF course the shooting ended; and as soon as they could get George Lawson on, he went up to the house with them, for he was too much cut up about the finding of the hand-kerchief, for Mr. Hamilton or Frank to trust him home at present. They must have some quiet talk with him, and keep him there till he was calmer, or it would have to come out; and then, all chance would be over of the old man mending. As it was, nothing could have been more fortunate, for as Charles had gone off to the sheep, and to see how the river was, the matter need be known but to themselves, if Lawson could only be induced to keep his counsel; and one thing was very certain, that they must not know at home, not even his mother; or, just as the excitement was dying down, it would all come up again as fresh as ever.

It was evident to Mr. Hamilton that the handkerchief must have been dropped where it was found, and dropped by Jessie—it was; when she crushed through the hedge and fell into the meadow down below; and it had lain there since, covered over by the snow which they dislodged; but how she got there, or why she was there, was hard to say. It was pretty clear, however, as nothing had been heard of her in the neighbourhood, that she must either have perished in the snow, in which case they might yet find her, or have fallen into the brook, which

there was deep ; or, as was most likely, mad-
dened by her father's curse—so strangely
heard, after an absence of so many years,
she had rushed off frantic, and had drowned
herself; and if so, the chances were she
had been swept on to the river.

However, they promised Lawson they
would themselves that evening, under the
plea of searching for "something lost,"
explore the brook the whole way to the
river ; and also, search well every drift they
came to. Meantime he must try to suppress
his feelings, and keep quiet ; and he had
much better leave the searching entirely to
them. It would only try him and could do
no good.

George Lawson, however, was not to be
put off so easily. He went with them; Mr.
Hamilton almost praying that their search
might be useless; for as more than a month
had elapsed since that fatal night, should

they find the poor girl, her body must be horribly disfigured, and they should then have the son in about as 'bad a state as the father.

Altogether, it was a terribly bad business, but they had to go through with it; and it was only when night came, and they had searched without result every drift in the wood, the fields, and the dingles, and had dragged and prodded all down the brook, right to the river, that Lawson would give in; and then the form the poor fellow was in was pitiable to see. He went off home to bed, and cried his heart out!

Frank, always up at six, went down next morning, and got George off. "We shall be out both together all to-day, Mrs. Lawson," said he, "and perhaps to-morrow, too. I want his help a bit about the farm." Thus matters were made safe for another day or two; during which time Frank and his father not only pressed upon George the absolute necessity of keeping the knowledge of "the find" from his father, but also showed him the utter absurdity and gross injustice of laying at Lewis's door Jessie's death, and all that had happened to her since she left her home.

True he had pestered her with his attentions, and had even threatened her, but that was years ago. "Aye, ten," said George, "when Jessie was eighteen; but were it ten times ten I'd make him suffer. He forced her off from Applepatch, and fired our ricks, and all but ruined us. No fault of his he didn't do it quite, but thanks to you, sir." "Come, come," said Hamilton, "now don't be rash. We cannot prove it; and, really, to lay this to him too—why, he may even not have seen her for some years! Be reasonable ; for were you by any chance to meet with him, it must come out; your

very quarrel would be sure to force it. Think
of your father, George, and let it rest."

"Yes, he thought of my poor sister, he
did, sir. However, he is my father, so it's
just as well. I can't curse him as he cursed
her that night. Poor soul! To think of her
back home that winter night, that bitter winter
night—for what? Her father's curse! Oh,
master, you don't know, sir, what I feel;
it makes me mad! Jessie and I got on so
well together, and so did mother; but
father, when drink was in him—well, he
was a brute! It's judgment, judgment,
what's come on him now!"

"Don't, don't, George, don't. It sounds
bad; he's your father." "He ought to
know it, sir," persisted George, "he ought."
"Well, if you tell him, you'll most likely
kill him." "I'll try not to. But if he
says a word, one word against her, if it's
years to come, why, he shall surely see

it. Here, here it is. There, read it—
'Jessie Jane'—there in the corner."

"I wish you would give that handkerchief to me; I would keep it for you,
Lawson." "It never leaves me," George
said, "now I've got it. It will serve, if
we should meet, to teach that scoundrel
Lewis how to read. I'll show him; oh,
yes, I'll show him 'Jessie Jane'—he liked
the name—and ask him if he knows now
where she is."

"I expect," said Frank, that night, when
with his father, "that some day soon there
will be a row down there. He is so
excited, feels it all so strongly, that the
slightest thing would make him blurt it
out. I wish we never had gone out that
day."

A few nights afterwards, when the snow
had nearly gone, George Lawson was again
in the enclosures, as he had been each

night; for the place seemed now to have some strange fascination for him, as though, with the rush of the water from the Welsh hills—that through the rapid thaw had made the river bank full, and was fast filling the streams — he should see his sister's body floating down the brook.

While there he heard a sound, a deadened sound, and noise of water; and as he stood to listen, the brook rushed by him swifter than before, then rose still higher; and as he still stood there, it came and splashed him. A louder sound, less deadened than before, and in a minute came a force of water that touched his knees, and nearly swept him over; and as he jumped upon the bank, it came there too.

He knew it now—the river bank had burst! He turned and ran; and as he went the bleat of sheep came to him through the roar, and changed his thoughts. They would all be drowned—yes, ewes and lambs! unless they could get to them, and that instantly. He jumped the next fence, and the next to that, and reached the wood, and raced along the drive, and, out of breath, was soon at Eymor House. The moon was up. He looked towards the meadows. One sheet of water!

Frank, soundly sleeping, dreamt there was a storm; he could hear it hailing. He woke and found the noise was at his window, Charles with the hethering—yes, that was it—batting against the panes. It was always kept there, handy in a corner, in case they wanted him. "Hillo! is that you, Charles— well, what's the matter now?" "Quick, Mr. Frank—the sheep! It is I, George Lawson. I think the bank has burst; they all are bleating. The moon is up, sir, if you'll get the glass." So out Frank tumbled, found the glass, and looked—he kept it on the shelf to sweep the fields in case of need, or any like alarm. "You are right, George; the water's in both meadows, and the hop-yard. Call Charles and William. The sheep as yet are safe; they are on the knoll, all huddled close together"—a raised bit in the meadow, made on purpose, for sudden floods; the river often rising in a night from twelve to twenty feet. "Can you see the white poles, sir?" said Lawson. "Yes, and a good height too, as yet, above the water. Tell them to saddle the old horse, and I'll be down directly."

"There's a mess with the sheep, father," said Frank, as he rapped at the door, on his way down-stairs. "Lawson is here, it seems the bank has burst. We are going to them." "All right," said Mr. Hamilton. "Save them if you can, my lad, but mind yourselves."

When Frank hurried down, and ran

round with George to the cart stable, Charles and William the waggoner were there ; the one, holding the tackle—always to be found in its place, in case of emergencies, and the other, putting a huge old saddle on " Captain," and digging him in the ribs to get the girths together; for Captain was a big, high horse, and the leader of the team, and it was not the first time by many that he had been so saddled. It was a rule at Eymor House that everything should be in its place, and provision made for all emergencies ; the consequence was, that whether it was an alarm of fire, a sudden need for the doctor, or accidents or ailments amongst the live stock in the fields, or the horses in the stables, not one there lost his head ; and the benefit of this was apparent, for loss of nerve meant always loss of time.

As Frank gave Lawson the long leggings

—two pairs of them, waterproof ones to the hips—for the men, and strapped a canvass bag round his own neck, the sound of bad language came to him. "There's that blackguard magpie on now," said he; "we have disturbed him, however. Oh, it's you, you young monkey, is it?" said Frank, as Tom made his appearance. "That varmint bird of yours always begins when he sees you." Tom slept with William and alongside Charles, by old Joe's room. "Now you go back to bed this very minute; we don't want you." "But a dunna waant to lose ma lamb, sur," said Tom. "Oh, bother the lamb," said Frank, alluding to one the lad had singled out as a special pet; "we'll see to all of them. Get back to bed." "Oh, sur, plase let ma come; a oona git i' the waay, sur, I oona; do, sur, plase." "Come along then, you young nipper; but understand, if you get into the water you must get out again : we shall have no time to look after you, I can tell you. Run on then, and get the gates open."

So down the bank they went, old Captain stepping each time he felt Frank's heels, and snorting like a war-horse at the water, when they turned in the meadow to the sheep; he knew his business, he had been there before.

Formerly the matter they had now on hand was managed in this way, as is still, indeed, the case on most farms. Men went into the water bodily, up to their hips, and often to their shoulders, and caught the swimming sheep and brought them out; but they used to lose the lambs, and sometimes the sheep, for the rush of the water was often so swift that to save themselves the men had frequently to let go when they had caught them. Two of their men had, moreover, been drowned, and several of them

had been laid up from time to time, through
being in the water; so three years ago, as
the lambing season came round, Frank be-
thought him of a little scheme, which was
tried and succeeded.

The means was a mound he made, some
eight or ten feet high, up in a corner, where
sheep could get and congregate together—the
river was low-bedded—and the appliances
were a travelling rope, with slings, stout
blocks and pulleys, four poles and staples,
and a canvass bag. The poles were fixtures,
permanently placed, two on the knoll, the
others opposite, just where the ground shelved
down to where it flattened. These poles
were painted white, and served as guides
at night, the straight way to them missing
all the ditches.

The tackle being fixed to the first poles,
was then taken through the water to the
others, and fixed there too; the padded

slings—two loops to each, with slip knots, straightened out, and a sheep caught. It was then held up on end, and the one loop slipped quickly round the shoulders at the back of the fore-legs, the other round the loins; the wide leather pad which occupied the space between the two keeping the loops apart, and preventing the cord cutting. Another ewe was then caught and secured in like manner, when the hauling-in of the off rope set them going through the water, the loops tightening with the weight of them. Released at the shore side, the tackle was then hauled in again, and the process repeated until all the ewes were caught.

The lambs fared better. A man—Frank, if at home—with a canvass bag slung round his neck, went through the water to them, on old Captain. Two lambs were caught, and tumbled in the bag, which then hung on the

saddle in the front, and was pushed sideways under the arm-pits, so that the arms
were free to steer the old horse back, while
the elbows kept the lambs in. As many
couples as there were of lambs, so many
splashings was it for the horse, just there
and back again. By this plan, as it prevented their struggles, the sheep and lambs
were more quickly rescued than by the old
one; besides which, it was safer for them and
safer for the men, who instead of having to
wade deep in the water, had then only
to get in it, just to push the sheep off;
one to give them a start while the other
hauled the rope.

"They are in for it at the mill," said
Frank, "for I can't hear the weir. By
Jove! we must look alive; there's no mistake about the bank now. Look how it's
coming!"

The scene was an exciting one. Trees in

the water, and a central point, whereon were sheep and lambs, all huddled there in terror. A backing of tall poplars and dark clouds. Around, a waste of water; white in the moonlight, but as red as marl. A swirl, a swish, a rush; a smacking of the flood against the bridge, a field beyond—a pause, a surging, and a pushing sound, as obstacles were met, or swept away. Big lumps of white foam, breadths of changing shadows, and great jagged branches sticking in the stream. The bleat of lambs, the answering cry of sheep, a hum of voices—caught for an instant, in a moment's calm—and shifting lights, as people out there, on the other side, saved what they could—the bank had burst there too. And as the clouds rolled on, a flood of light, that showed the boiling, bounding, leaping water, still coming to them through a clean-cut gap, which slanting withies showed was widening.

"That's it," said Frank, as William fixed the tackle, "give him a leg up, will you, George;" and with the wagoner behind him, hold of the rope, Captain, carrying double, soon took them to the other side, the water wetting him above his girths. The man slipped off and fastened up the cords, and Frank went back again and then brought Charles, as George was there to liberate the sheep, and Tom to tend them.

"Stop a bit," said Frank, "and we'll tell them over. It may be some are lost." "A han told 'em, sur," said the wagoner. "And what do you make the tale of 'em then?" "Siven-an-forty, sur," said William. "Noineteen lambs, an aight-an-twenty ship." "That's right, then, for the rest are by the house, so now let's go to work." "That ool be fourteen twos fur we, sur, an noine fur you—noine an a harf. Ull do it now a think, sur, an look aloive. It conna roise

quick wi' the breadth it han; an as long as
the oud hos con keep his back aboove the
waater, ween be roight; and when he conna
we mun ha' a swim."

"There you are, sir," said Charles, who
had no brogue about him. "Two little
beauties, and Tom's is one of 'em, so that 'll
put him right and make him peaceable," and
as Frank kept them in with his elbows, and
took them over, Charles and the wagoner
slung the ewes; old Captain, as he returned,
snorting loudly each time, as they travelled
by him—two moving heaps of fleeces. In
less time than many would suppose, the
flock was landed, with the exception of one
ewe and two lambs, that were swept away
through straying—the lambs being frightened
and the ewe following them—and not seen
till it was too late; Frank and the men
getting back again the same way they went.

"Keep them together now, Tom," said

Frank, "and well from the water; don't let us have our trouble over again, my lad." "No, meyster," said Tom, as he circled them to keep them to the dry part and get them in a line with the gate, " but this here littler un, sur, o' moine he be a ronk un; uz on a cuttin caapers!" "Look after him then, or I shall make you cut 'caapers.' There! you stupid, young beggar, look there," said Frank, as Tom switched the youngster, and he, being an impulsive lamb, at once jumped away and tumbled in the ditch, and was sailing down it before either of them could reach him. "You want your young head broken, you do. See after him, William, or he'll be through the hedge and we shall lose him."

But the lamb was the one Tom had singled out for a pet a week ago—he went in for pets and had some young wild rabbits one time and some birds another—so he jumped into

the ditch after him, full as it was, and, as
a matter of course, with the pace the water
was then rushing there, he and the lamb
too, got hurried to the hedge, where he
caught him; but after hanging to him for
a minute, they were both swept through
the briars into the hop-yard, to the great
detriment of the lad's features.

"Hold on yourself, and let him go!"
cried Frank, as both went sailing on for
where the flood came. "Let go, I say;
you young dog, you'll be drowned. Quick,
William!" "A dunna car, a oona let 'im
goo. A manes ta have 'im." "Let go,
and catch the poles, you young imp, you.
You'll be drowned. D'ye hear?" "A dunna
car," cried Tom; "ef a bin drownded, a
knowst theest mind ma maggit. A aint
agwain ta lose him, bless his heart. He's
worth a pound, or more!"

Frank, who was still mounted, said "hit

him, George, for I must reach that lad, our
man will miss him." So with the tackle,
Lawson laid on stoutly, which so astonished
Captain, that he bolted, and jumped the
hedge, as Frank then wished him to; but
before Tom could be reached, the horse
swerved sideways right into the water, and
getting in the ditch—that there went down
the middle of the hop-yard—he came to
grief, fell, threw Frank, and then plunged
into deep water, and was swept down
with it.

Knowing Frank could swim, and letting
the horse take his chance, George, leaving
Charles with the sheep, ran round to the
hop-yard, and got on by the hedge; but
fast as he went, he would have been too late,
had not it been for a big old withy, brought
down there by the flood, that had lodged
against the yew-tree at the bottom. Tom
drifted down close by it, and got hold, and

held on stoutly; then scrambled up and stood upon the withy; when, pushing up the lamb into the yew, where was a landing, and a good strong fork, he climbed up after him, and there sat grinning—he was safe at last. George waded in the water to his waist, took off the lamb, and then Tom on his shoulders. Frank got off with a wetting, and got out; and Captain, after he had had a good swim, which he seemed thoroughly to enjoy, turned round and got out too, and came to William.

"What could you ‚have been thinking of?" said Frank, as he stood there dripping, "you nearly lost your life, you young monkey, and gave me a bath into the bargain." "Is sur," was Tom's reply, "but uz gotten the lamb, ud a niver a loosed him, bless him." "Yes, but I think you thought more of that confounded old magpie than you did of your life." "But he be a proper bird, he

be, sur." "A most improper one, you mean;
but as you have shown some pluck, and it
will perhaps turn your thoughts from that
abominable bird, you may keep the lamb
and pet that."

So Tom did pet him; called him "Flood,"
and made him follow him all about the farm
and lie down by him in the saddle room;
Peterkin resenting it from his cage by calling
Tom and the lamb all manner of names,
whenever he saw them.

After Frank had changed his things and
breakfasted, and Lawson had done likewise,
they got the boat from the pool and took it
down in the cart, and stayed there till the
afternoon, rowing about the meadows and
the hop yard, the flood having then risen
above the hedges. They hoped to find the
ewe, to save the fleece, but ewe and lambs
had been washed down the river. They
caught some fish though, and a whacking

pike, that was stuck fast in the hedge; and after the flood went down they got lots of eels too in the hop-yard alleys.

In the evening Minchem of the Hawthorns came up—a tall, gaunt, sallow man, with a strongly featured face, his nose and his mouth being on speaking terms, to know particulars, and to have his growl.

"Yes," said Mr. Hamilton, "but it might have been worse." "Worse! ah, that's what you always say." "So it might; we might have lost them all." "Look at your big meadow, all under water. It will be mud, John, mud!" "Yes, I hope it will, a fine alluvial deposit, and worth money. It will fertilise the land, and bring big swathes at mowing." "Your hop-yard, too; I saw the poles there swimming, the stacks upset." "Yes, it will give the men some work, they have had none lately; and what the flood leaves, will, James, force the hops."

"But see the gap it's made!" "Which will be mended. It might have given when the hay was down, and all the lot of it lodged on the hops. It was so one year, and that without a burst." "That ewe and two lambs lost—a double couple!" "For which the benefit will more than pay—we shall make it up at hay-making and picking."

"Ah!" said Minchem despondingly, "it is no use my talking to you, John, I can see." "Not in the grumbling line, that's very certain," said Mr. Hamilton. "If a man is gifted with common sense, has his proper quantity of brains, and is blessed with health, he should exert himself, put his own shoulder to the wheel, and take ordinary precautions against those ills that happen, and not blame Providence for every incident, while he himself looks on, with both hands deep down in his breeches pockets. James, I'm ashamed of you, you ought to know better. God bless the man! do have some self-reliance."

"But you have such nerve, John, such wonderful nerve," pleaded Jemmy. "Nerve? stuff, nonsense! Make up your mind to a thing and you'll do it. Your timid, weakly atom of a man is worse by far than your loud blusterer. The one may gain by very confidence, the other fail because he's like a mouse. You'll excuse me, won't you?" "Oh, we never quarrel, never; do we, John? we only differ." "And leave off friends; so come and have a pipe."

The ladies too came up — the Misses Minchem, his sisters, Tabitha and Angelina —he was a bachelor.

Tabitha was forty - three — four years younger than her brother—but she owned to thirty. She was a pale, thin-faced, thin-lipped personage, with an aggressive nose, red as to the end of it; and hard and

bony too, about the jaws; and with shifting restless eyes, that were always taking
stock of you, but which, when observed,
were removed instantly; such removal being
followed in an unconcerned sort of a manner,
by two sniffs and a wink, of a pronounced
character. She was tall and gaunt, like
her brother.

Angelina was more truthful, if spiteful;
for though she was but thirty-eight, she
owned to thirty-five, so as to take prece-
dence of her elder sister. She also was tall
and spindley, and she had a full and florid
face, and a mole by the right ear; bold
eyes that could stand looking at, and a com-
pressed mouth, that had an unpleasant habit
of saying rude things in a sarcastic manner.

Both sisters sat upright—very much so—
and in any conversation with them, Tabitha's
sniffs were distinctly audible. They took

cake and wine with equal eagerness, and a
second or a third glass too, when offered
them; drinking your health in the first
with an old-fashioned politeness, though in
a sinister sort of way, and setting down
the glass with a gasp, and a slight pushing
of the chair backwards, as though it were
a disagreeable task well got over.

They were cute maidens, both of them;
and before they had done with you, what
they came to know, they generally did know,
for they were great in tactics, and wonderful at scandal. Young men they always con-
demned as "a bad lot," just as a set-off for
their lack of discrimination in allowing them,
the Misses Minchem, to remain so long in
single blessedness; while old maids were
designated "worthy creatures," to favour the
idea that they too preferred a single life, to
do good deeds. Tabitha and Angelina too,

very often deceived themselves, but they seldom deceived other people.

They were often at the Hamiltons, but they were not welcome visitors, for they had never a good word to say about any one; so Nelly did not like them, nor did her mother; for they were like the old man, their brother, who came with a grumble and who left with a sneer. The object of their present visit was to pick up all they could about old Lawson, and "that white face," but what the Hamiltons did know they kept to themselves.

A week later, however, an event happened that all in Eymor knew, so the precautions taken were at once rendered useless.

Things turned out as expected. The old man's cunning strengthened day by day. He taunted them. "'Twas false, he had found them out. He knew it now, they both were leagued against him. There was no face, it was nothing but the moon. He curse his daughter? No, it was a lie! to make him change his mind and have her home."

"It is no lie!" cried George, "she had come back home—God best knows how—and looked in at the window; but you—you drove her from it with a curse—a curse!"

"A lie, a lie! You don't get over me. Your proof, your proof?"

"See here, we stopped it up—this brick-work's new!" and up he dragged his father to the wall. "And here's her handkerchief! Read, read it, 'Jessie Jane.' You cursed her, killed her; her body's in the water!" With that he flung him back into his chair.

Old Lawson from that day continued childish.

CHAPTER XIII.

SHADE AND SUNSHINE—JESSIE LAWSON.

WHEN Jessie, as the sound of the weir came
to her, staggered across the road in the
direction of it on the night of New Year's
eve, to rush on to the river, and so end all her
troubles in the water, the blinding snow
half hid a heap of stones, placed by the rails
there at the Bridge Lane corner. She came
upon it, tripped, and then fell heavily—a
fall that saved her; for though help seemed
furthest from her, help was nigh. She lay
there, stunned.

"Putt the slipper on, John," said Betsy

Plummer, as she and her good-man—old-fashioned homely folks—reached the end of the downs, and came to the long steep road that thence went down to Eymor, "this last load be a heavy un, and mebbe it ool run thun osses, the groun be slithery." "Now dunna thee bother, Betsy; theer be no fear; it baint harf slithery it!" "But it ool be bym by, when the snow shuts, an it catches hup a bit." "Well, that binna it, be it? Conna yer see how it be a keepin on? Toime enough when they begins to slither. Come hup! Duke. Hammer him, Betsy; dunna yer note how Duchess be a pullin? That's it," said he, as she administered punishment with an exaggerated umbrella of the Gamp type, "dunna spar him. Duke, yer stoopid! darn yer oud body, yer got it now." "Look yer theer," said Mrs. Plummer, as Duke jumped and started, "a knowst theest brake my neck! Now putt the slipper on, John, or Ise jump out." "What a botherin oud ooman thee bist, Betsy; thee isseht agwain to be hurt, ist tha?" "Jump down," said Betsy, "a oona goo a peerk further ooth yer, ef tha dussent, theer now, a oona!" "Bother the ooman," said John, as he got down and did it. "Now thin," said he, as he stepped into the wagon again and brought the snow with him, "thee be quoiet, an be asy. Thee bist oonder coover, an warm—whaat more dost tha waant?" and relapsing into silence, the pair went down the hill steadily.

"That be 'good-boye' to you," said John, as they reached the bottom. "A hopes a shanna see your oud faace agin fur a longful toime, fur Ise comed up an down yer long enough." "Well, God send us no worse luck, John," said Betsy, "an thin we shanna hurt. A hopes William be a gotten saafe wi the big load, an landed;

an wese git on comfortable loike an paceable ooth him, and pull togither, all on us, fur a livin."

The one to whom Mrs. Plummer alluded was her son-in-law, George Jenkins; who, having married her daughter some twelve years ago, was now, by dint of good luck and industry, well off, and tenant of a little farm, whereon were sheep, a rick or two, and cows—a farm in Warwickshire; and he and his wife, therefore, wished the old people to come and be with them, as the house was a roomy one, and they could all live there together. So they were now on their way to Wellesbourne, with the last load of goods from the Farm-Fold, Bromyard.

"Keep tha quoiet, Betsy," said John, "whoile a walks 'em; the Gaaite be open— ween gie Will Ford the slip."

The feat being accomplished, and the toll saved—through the foresight of a wild night,

by the man at the turnpike, and his disin-
clination to turn out "on a rough un"—
John took off the slipper and jogged on
noiselessly; for the snow which had here
and there been blown off the banks, lay
thickly on the levels.

"Theya be loighted hup a see," said Betsy,
as they passed the shop; "a oonder whaat's
agate?" "Twins," said John, "an Purdey
off his yud." "Git hout!" said Betsy; "it
be a poor yud to goo off at that. A dunna
belave it." "Well, it ba possible, baint it?
Hur's had 'em oonst, as I knows on, an so
han others too, in Eymor." "The nuts, an
the lambs, John, that wan it, bunches an
double couples, lots on 'em. But they wan
scaarce last year, so that baynt loikely; not
ef so be as her toime be come, which it
moight or it moighter not—we dunna kneow,
how shoon us? Dunna thee go romancin,
John, o' sich things, it be wicked."

"Theer! a knowd it," said Betsy, as a low moan caught her ear, "that be judgment, that be, fur saayin what wanna true. Theer agin! Conna thee hear it? O John! Lard bless us and saave us, what ool become on us? Yer oughter not, yer know. O lar, O lar! do putt me somewheer saafe!" and Betsy crept from the seat to the centre, and looked about her for some place of security among the crocks and chattels.

"Whoy thee oud stupid," said John, whose sense of hearing, through gouty twinges, was less acute that Betsy's, "thee bist off thee yud too, bissint tha? Whaat ails tha? Come hup, Duke!" but Duke declined to come up when he hit him, and pressing up to Duchess, pricked his ears. "It be the smell o' the male fro' the mill," said John; "he'd wind a bane a moile off."

But there was more in it evidently than bean-meal, though John was oblivious to it;

for Duke put his head down and snorted,
and kept peering before him, quite careless
as to proceeding. "Come hout o' that ! do,"
said John, "yer frightened oud ooman, you,
an houd the reins. Yer maakes ma savage,
yer do. A mun git down a bit, Duke's feet
be ball'd," so Betsy had to come to the front
again. "Consume the snow, ween nivver
git to Ooster !" "Don't be a fool, Betsy,"
said John presently, as he looked up at her
sternly, with the pick in his one hand, and
Duke's foot in the other. "Dun yer think a
be saft ? Yer conna froighten me, yer conna!
Whatn yer do it fur thin ? A dunna loike
sich souns. Drap 'em !" and John pecked
at the foot again, and then picked up the
other. "It wanna me, no it wanna," was
Betsy's answer. "Come into the waggin
agin, or Ise loose the reins. A oona spy
the road not no more; no, not fur fifty
pouns. Theer be sperrits about !" "A knows

theer be," laughed John, "both rum an brandy. Goo in an hev a drap," and Betsy vanished.

"The Lord be merciful to us," cried John, as some one moaned, "whatever wan it? By gom but hur said true," and looking round he heard a moan again. Now this was awkward, for after John's brag of courage, it would ill become ·him then to play the coward; so he caught fast hold of Duke and Duchess, and stood between them, to wait events; wishing, but not daring to say so, that his wife Betsy would jump down and look about there, while he pretended to be quite unable then to leave the horses. But Betsy was safely housed, and meant to be.

Another moan! and John looked to the lane; and there upon a mound was something living, all black and white, that moved and swayed, and moved and swayed again, till he, unable to keep quiet longer, cried "Jump down, Betsy! fur Ise wery bad;" at which the thing so peckledy, sat up on end, and looked at him, so he at once subsided, and Betsy found him trembling like a leaf. "Come in," said she, "now do, an hev a drap; it be the cold, a knows, it's brought the shivers. Theest hev the colic ef tha don't jump up."

"Please help me!" said a voice, and that a woman; and John and Betsy both looked at each other. "Please help me, do!" "It's there," said John, "on that hape by the corner. Some ooman lost." "A ooman!" Betsy said, and went straight to it—in woman's sympathy forgetting fear.

"Poor soul," said she, as kneeling down by Jessie, she raised her up and put her arms around her, "John, bring the lantern and some brandy here—be quick! Look up, my lass, it all be roighted now. Ween see yer saafe. Youm perished wi' the cold. How come it all? Youm whoited wi' the snow." "I lost my way," said Jessie, very faintly. "An wheer bist gwain, an wheer wast comin from, an wheer be all your frens, whaat be yer naame?" said Mrs. Plummer to her in a breath. "Weem come fro' Bromyard wi' a load o' things. 'Twas lucky fur tha. Here, lass," said she, as John came with the brandy, "now tak a soop, it ool do tha good. A little drap, now troy. Ef theest be gwain our waay, ween tak tha on to Ooster."

"Worcester?" said Jessie, with faint voice, and slowly. "Is, Ooster," Betsy said, "Come drink it hup, ween tak yer in the waggin, saafe enough, or ef theest loike to staay here till it's loight, ween call em up theer at t' Eymor Arms—it's welly six—to tak tha in; or thee cost goo to Ooster 'long o' us."

"Oh, Worcester, Worcester, please—with

you, with you," said Jessie. "It was so cruel! so very very cruel!" "Come, one sup more, ma lass, an don't thee bother, an thin ween pick tha hup, an putt tha in the waggin, snug an waarm. Ween be theer well to breakfast, con we hurry."

"Yes, hurry, do please hurry," Jessie said, inclined to wander, "or he may curse me." "Cuss tha, ma lass, not I," said John, "uz waaite yer toime. Ween bate upon the road, ef comes to that. Weem gwain to Brummagen, but not till evenin; to-morrer on to Warwick, to live beyand it. Wellesbourne. Dost know it?" "Here, gie a hand, said Betsy, "an houd thee bother. Conna yer see as how her inna roight? The cold ha' struck her, an bin ta much fur her. Her's off her yud, an quare, her's muttrin. Now I ool take her one futt an the tother, you catch her shouders. Ween git her in atween us that awaay."

And so they carried her, and laid her down inside with care, and gently.

"Now fetch the lantern an git on apace, or ween be laate." "A ool," said Plummer, "for the snow's a shuttin. It be welly over;" and Eymor soon was many miles behind them.

Through warmth and stimulus, poor Jessie slept—slept all the way, tired out; and when they woke her, at the journey's end, at half-past eight, she still was dreaming—in spite of frequent catchings of her breath, and hand at side—dreaming of Landimoor, and happier days, with friends at Upperton.

When Plummer pulled up at "The Farmer's Arms" near to the station, to stay till evening, then on, with horses rested, he lifted Jessie out, and got the landlady, a portly looking dame, a friend of theirs, to see to her, and tend her for a while, till she could travel. He had found her by the road, he said, as they came in. He would pay the cost if she would take the trouble.

"We'll talk of that, John Plummer, when you're richer. I'll see to her," was Mrs. Goode's reply. With that she had her taken up to bed; she saw she needed it, and the two old people breakfasted together.

"That poor girl's very ill," said Mrs. Goode, when they came in to dinner some hours after. "The doctor's coming soon, to see our Lizzie; he sees her daily. I'll get him look at her; I think it's fever. She's hot and cold and wanders off at times, and very thirsty. It's just the way that Lizzie was took first, barring that catching at the side she's got. D'ye know about her?"

"No," John said, "a knowst nothin but whaat a telda. We fund her on a hape o' stones by Eymor Mill. Her's some poor lass as arnt got not no frens, a taake it. Poor ooman! but Ise sorry. Ise do ma part ef yer con better her. Don't send her to the 'Firmary or Workhus. Her's better bred, a think—her hands be saft."

"You leave it all to me, John, I'll see to her. Here is the doctor." "Well, whaats a saay?" said John, when she came down. "She's feverish, and needs both care and quiet. She's very ill. He thinks 'tis pleurisy that's coming on." "Then her mun waaite, a taake it. Poor wench, poor wench!" "Yes, for if that pain gets worse, he'll have to bleed her. He asked her if she felt it like a knife, but she said 'no.'" "'She will, though, I expect,'" said he, "'I'll look in soon.'"

Having to start at four, both John and Betsy asked if they might see her, but she was sleeping, so they went away, Mrs. Goode promising to give her their message, and to write to them.

When the doctor came again, the symptoms of pleurisy were decisive—the "knife" was there—so it had to be at once combated with the lancet. "She must be kept quiet," said the doctor, "for I shall have to put her at once under the influence of tartar-emetic, Mrs. Goode, and combine it too with a little calomel, neither of them strengthening things, as you well know by Jenny,"—her youngest girl, who suffered from the croup; "therefore, as you decide to keep her here, you must make up your mind for a fortnight of it, certainly, it may be longer; I cannot say, at present, as we don't yet know to what influences, besides to cold and exposure, she has been subjected. It was a bitter night, I know, for I was out in it—Mrs. Dallow of Ombersley; a boy again. That made me past my time with you this morning."

When Jessie found how things were, and

that she must be still and patient, and stay there for some time, she took her purse from underneath the pillow, and gave it to the landlady.

It contained money, a key, and a left-luggage ticket, and her box was fetched from the station; Jessie having left it there late overnight, when she went on by the Malvern line—as she would have five miles to walk from where she was set down, and she did not then know how they would receive her at home, after so many years of absence. If favourably, she had no doubt she could get the box by the carrier in a day or two; if otherwise, she would return and take it.

She timed her arrival at Landimoor for ten o'clock, when she knew her father would be most likely to be out; and as they never went to bed there on New Year's Eve until they had seen "the Old Year out and the New Year in," by that arrangement she might perhaps get an hour or two alone with her mother—who was always kind to her—before he came. She missed her way though, and it made her later, and it was nearly midnight when she reached the bridge.

It was soon enough, however—too soon, perhaps—for all she met with was a father's curse.

"I'm very ill," said Jessie; "keep the key. What things I have, you'll find there in the box."

Upon the box was "Paddington to Worcester.—J. Jane." Within it were some clothes, each marked "J. J.;" a book or two, and likenesses—three photos—one was her own, a baby in her arms; another a man— a gentleman—with brush and palette; the third, a child, a curly-headed boy.

For quite a week her state was critical, and then the worst was over. She had a

mother's care from Mrs. Goode, who failed
to know, however, more about her; for,
finding questioning did but distress her, she
ceased to try for further information. She
knew but this—and that by accident, when
Jessie wished to pay her for her trouble—
that all she had of money in the world was
in that purse — a very slender store—four
pounds was all. She gave her back the purse,
and saw the doctor. "I cannot charge her,
after what you say," said he; and so he
saw her, and gave her all she needed, free of
cost; as did the landlady, who insisted on it.

Another week of good nursing, found her
safe—from a relapse at least—but weak and
low; when all at once, she said that she
must go—go then and there, that day, that
afternoon—aye, up to town. The doctor
spoke in vain; her kind nurse too; go then
she must. She gave no reason, other than
she must; she "felt" she must.

Therefore, as they both found that she was determined, they each gave her a note —the doctor to a brother of his, a hospital surgeon, in case she needed aid ; and Mrs. Goode, a line or two to her sister, at Pentonville, who might, she said, be of some use to her, should she want a friend.

So she went ; Mrs. Goode seeing her off, paying for her ticket—for she was one of the Good Samaritans of this world—and speaking to the guard about her—" but I only did," said she, " as I'd be done by."

When Jessie got out at Paddington, and was looking for her luggage, a gentleman who had got in at Oxford, and who was standing by her, said, " That's mine, porter, ' Anderson,' portmanteau ; " and turning quickly to hail a cab, he brushed against her. " I beg your pardon," said he.

" Harry !" " Jenny !" were their mutual exclamations, as he raised his hat, and their eyes met; and then shaking hands warmly with each other, he passed his arm through hers, and drew her from the throng. " Oh Harry," Jessie said, " I could not find you. Thank God we meet again! I felt we should." " Yes; I wrote, but you had left; the letter was returned. I am so very glad once more to see you." " But I hope you are not ill?" said he, seeing Jessie falter. " Lean on my arm a bit. Where is the child ?"

" In heaven I hope—our baby boy is dead ! I have lost my all. I have now no friend—not one !" " Oh, Jenny, don't say that, now I am with you. We always were friends, and we always will be—and now, we must be. Where are you living ? Let me see you home."

" I have no home," and Jessie burst out crying. " No home ! Then come with me; I'll find a home. Cheer up now, don't you cry! Come, trust in me; I'll see what can be done. Stay here a moment."

"No, not a cab—four-wheeler I want now —portmanteau and that box." And Jessie got in, Harry got in too; and as they drove away, she once more smiled.

The shade had passed — 'twas sunshine once again!

END OF VOL I.

CHARLES DICKENS AND EVANS, CRYSTAL PALACE PRESS.

Milton Keynes UK
Ingram Content Group UK Ltd.
UKHW040139160224
437928UK00003B/31

9 783382 828578